THE
MISFITS
CLUB

THE MISFITS CLUB

CLUB

KIERAN CROWLEY

FEIWEL AND FRIENDS
NEW YORK

A FEIWEL AND FRIENDS BOOK
An imprint of Macmillan Publishing Group, LLC
175 Fifth Avenue, New York, NY 10010

Our books may be purchased in bulk for promotional, educational, or business use. Please contact your local bookseller or the Macmillan Corporate and Premium Sales Department at (800) 221-7945 ext. 5442 or by e-mail at MacmillanSpecialMarkets@ macmillan.com.

Library of Congress Control Number: 2017944815

ISBN 978-1-250-07926-8 (hardcover) / ISBN 978-1-250-07927-5 (ebook)

Book design by Carol Ly

Feiwel and Friends logo designed by Filomena Tuosto

First edition, 2018

10 9 8 7 6 5 4 3 2 1

mackids.com

FOR MY PARENTS, MARY AND DAN

ONE

"**Y**ou're dead."

The thing nobody had ever told Brian about being chased was that it was fun. It was terrifying, too, but that was part of the fun. Of course, the fact that he was on a bicycle, his trusty old Stringer White 5000, meant that he had an advantage over the two idiots who were after him; they were on foot. He flipped the pedals backward, using the rear brakes to send the bike into a curving skid that spat up gravel chips from the churchyard.

It was almost one o'clock, eighteen days to the end of summer vacation and fifteen days to the end of the Misfits Club. A large gray-white cloud was beginning to hide the early afternoon sun as Brian straightened up the bike. On one side of him was the town of Newpark, on the other a road that bisected the town's largest housing development. Beyond that lay the countryside and his escape.

"Did you hear me?" the bigger of his two pursuers shouted.

"I wasn't really listening. Was it something about being dead?"

His mother had said that he had a smart mouth, just like his dad—the only thing they had in common, Brian hoped—and that smart mouths got you into trouble. She was right about that; he was often in trouble.

Of course, he'd be in more trouble if these two hairy gorillas caught up with him. Gorilla number one was flabby and out of shape and not that much of a threat. Gorilla number two was a different prospect, though. He was younger and fitter and he wasn't issuing threats. In fact, he wasn't saying anything at all. That freaked Brian out a little bit. His father had always warned him that the quiet ones were the ones you had to watch out for.

The gap between them was about fifty yards. Unless one of them was an Olympic sprinter, there was no way he was going to be caught.

"You're so dead they'll have to bury you twice," the heavier of the two men roared.

Brian faked a yawn, really exaggerated it, too. "Sorry, did you say something? You're so far away it's hard to hear you."

He thought gorilla number one was going to explode with rage. His cheeks puffed out and his face began to turn crimson, from the tip of his forehead to the bottom of his chin—dazzlingly red—like it was the world's worst superhero power. It made Brian smile until he realized that he'd lost sight of the second guy. There was no sign of him. Had he just given up?

VRRRROOOM.

Uh-oh, Brian thought. *That's not the sound of someone giving up.* It was actually the sound of a car, a cobalt-blue 2004 Subaru Impreza, to be completely accurate. A souped-up car, if the roaring, guttural engine sounds that sent great rumbling tremors across the ground were anything to go by. It emerged from the hidden parking space on the side of Colbert Street like a predator emerging from the undergrowth.

"Oh crud," Brian said as his stomach lurched.

He was quick on the bike, but he didn't think he was quicker than an Impreza. He was about to find out for certain. The car revved, took off, then stopped briefly to let the bigger guy climb in as Brian spun the bike around by the handlebars, stood up, and began pedaling faster than he ever had before.

There was a left turn thirty yards ahead that led into a cul-de-sac. If he could get to the end of the cul-de-sac, he could make it over the Hennigans' back wall and disappear into the maze of alleys behind their house. They'd never find him there.

The left turn was only ten yards away now. Another plan was beginning to form in Brian's brain.

Form faster, form faster, he thought.

The car closed the distance between them quickly and the nose of the Impreza was just behind him as he turned into the cul-de-sac at full speed, leaning low, his shoulder almost grazing the ground as the bike struggled to stay on two wheels.

Brian was almost parallel to the tarmac, but he was in the flow—completely focused, nothing existing outside of him and this moment. Time slowed. He could see everything all at once, hear the noise of children playing, smell the fumes from the car's giant exhaust, then the whine as the car struggled to follow him into the turn.

The back end of the car swung wide, dragging the rest of the vehicle with it, followed by the look of sheer panic on the bigger man's face as he briefly thought they were going to smack into a wall. The younger man corrected the spin with two sharp movements of the steering wheel. The car righted itself with a judder.

Brian launched himself onto the small green, and circled around, digging a tire track in the soft grass, before heading back in the goons' direction. He knew he wouldn't make it to the Hennigans' house before they caught him. It was time for Plan B.

As they watched, openmouthed, he briefly considered making a rude gesture, but instead he just waved. It was hard to tell because he was traveling at full speed, but they appeared to be getting even angrier.

He didn't want to head back toward town—they'd catch him too easily—so there was only a single possibility left. It was one he didn't want to take because it depended on how lazy a neighbor had been over the last few days, but he decided that he had no other choice. The other possibilities, ones that involved him begging for mercy or shouting for someone to call the cops, never occurred to him.

The turn-off was on the opposite side of the road, past the housing development. He was nearly there when he heard the car's tires squeal as it joined him on the main road.

He veered the bike right again, down a narrow path with grass growing in the middle. The end of the housing development was on one side, nothing but fields on the other. Brian hoped that the farmer who owned the fields hadn't gotten around to fixing the broken fence yet. It sagged down next to the iron gate at the end of the path, leaving an opening of about three feet, enough of a gap for Brian and the bike to make it through if he was careful, but not enough space for a car to follow. Brian pedaled furiously. The adrenaline that had kept him going was running out now—his lungs were on fire and his legs felt like concrete, but he kept pedaling. He was only feet away when the car loomed up behind him.

He was going to make it.

As he slipped between the tumbledown barbed-wire fence and the concrete post of the iron gate, he saw that it was padlocked. He heard the screech of brakes as the car tried to avoid slamming into the gate. He'd done it. Even if they tried to break the lock, he'd be miles away from them by the time they managed it. The only way they could chase him now was by running after him, and he knew they wouldn't do that. They'd never catch him on foot.

He glanced behind and saw both of them standing by the car. The bigger guy was shaking his fist and shouting something at him. Something rude, no doubt, but Brian couldn't hear it.

They'd given up. He was free. Or at least he would have been if he'd been paying attention.

The grassy field wasn't the smoothest of surfaces and as he bounced along the rutted path he hit something, a rock maybe, nothing he could clearly see. It jolted the bike and sent him flying over the handlebars. He hit the ground hard, scudded along the surface for a couple of seconds before he came to a stop, twisted on his side.

"Ow," he said.

Ow was a little bit of an understatement. It hurt a lot more than an *ow*'s worth. He heard one of the men laugh, a hollow mocking laugh that really annoyed him, nearly as much as the severe pain he was in annoyed him.

Brian clambered to his feet. The men had taken a few steps into the field. He was in no shape to outrun them. He wasn't even sure he could reach his bike in time.

"We've got him now," one of them said.

AMELIA'S JOURNAL

6pm—Everything is sort of normal. If you think a screaming baby and a house being in a complete mess is normal. It's been like that for the last six weeks since Susanna, Her Royal Highness, first arrived. Six weeks old and my new baby sister is already the center of the universe and now it's like I don't exist at all. Twelve years of being an only child and suddenly they've forgotten about me. It's not fair. It really isn't. I get that she's small and, when her face isn't all red and scrunched up 'cause she's crying (which is never), she is kind of cute, but why does she have to get all the attention?

7:15pm—Everything is HORRIBLE. More horrible than being forgotten. I hate my dad and I hate my stepmother. During dinner they tricked me into thinking everything was okay by acting all nice to me and stuff. They said having a new baby around was tough on me, but it was also tough on everybody else. They said they were glad I was helping out (I wasn't doing that much) and then they gave me a gift card as a present. For one complete second I was actually happy. Then after dessert they sat down and put on sad voices and I'm-sorry faces and said there was something we needed to talk about. Except that there wasn't anything to talk about because they'd already decided everything. All because of a little joke!

And now here I am, writing in this stupid journal with its stupid flowers on the stupid cover for the first time in four years. I don't even like writing, but I have to do something right now or else I'll just EXPLODE! I can't even talk to any of my friends because my dad took away my phone and tablet for the night when I got mad and woke the baby up. I still can't believe what's happening. They're making me move out of my own home! Where I've lived all my life, while my stepmother gets to stay here even though she's only lived here for three years. HOW IS THAT FAIR? I don't want to move. I like my friends. I like my room. I like my life, or I did until Susanna arrived. They say it's only for summer vacation until things calm down with Her Royal Highness, but how can I trust them? My dad is kicking his own daughter out of her own home!

When Vivienne and my dad got married she was nice to me. Always taking me to fun places. On Saturday nights, we'd get takeout and she'd make hot chocolate and we'd sit on the couch watching The X Factor.

"I'm not just your stepmother—I'm your friend," she used to say. But what she's doing now isn't very friendly, is it?

I have to live with my GRANDMOTHER! I don't want to live with my grandmother. Don't get me wrong, Gran's nice to me, but she's not exactly what you'd call normal—unless you think things like shouting at crows or singing so loudly the neighbors can hear are normal. I don't. She lives over thirty miles away and I won't see my friends all summer. I've never been left on my own with Gran before, so that's going to be completely strange, and my bedroom in her farm-house smells old and musty. Gran likes reading all these books I've never heard of, and she doesn't even own a computer. What if she makes me milk a cow or something? I don't like cows. They stare at you the whole time, like they're plotting something sinister. And the town she lives near is nothing like my hometown. It's a really odd place. I'm not a snob, but the people there are different, kind of weird and some of them smell. Everything's going to be AWFUL.

TWO

Brian did the first thing that popped into his head. He pretended he'd become faint and flopped to the ground. It was a bit overdramatic and he wouldn't have won an Oscar for it—in fact, his performance would have been booed on many stages—but it was all that came to mind. After falling off his bike, he wasn't in any condition to outrun the gorillas who were following him.

He hoped that they'd just turn around and drive away, but of course they didn't do that. He hadn't heard them walking through the soft grass, so he was lucky he didn't jump when he heard their voices close by.

"Is he dead?" one of them asked.

Brian kept his eyes shut tight. He tried to keep his breathing as shallow as possible.

"He'd better not be. I don't want to end up in prison. Not again."

"He fell off his bike. We didn't do anything. We're innocent."

"You know how them lawyers twist things around. They'll make out that it was all our fault. They'll say we were trying to rob that shop when all we did was forget our wallets and they'll say we were putting this stupid kid in danger when we were just messing around. He was the one who started the chase."

"I hate lawyers."

"Maybe we should check if he's dead."

The bigger guy, gorilla number one, poked at Brian's back with the toe of his sneaker. Brian groaned a little.

"He's alive," the smaller one said, sounding relieved.

"Should we give him CPR?"

"What? Are you nuts? We're not touching him. Fingerprints and all that. No, we're getting out of here. The sooner we're on the road, the better." He leaned over and spoke into Brian's ear. "If anyone asks you questions about today, you say nothing, right? You never saw us."

Brian groaned again.

The guy took the groan as a sign of agreement. He stood up.

"Let's get out of here before we get in trouble," the big guy said, stomping his way back to the car and bellowing in despair when one of his fancy sneakers landed in a present a cow with a nervous stomach had left behind in the field.

Brian kept his eyes shut until he heard the car racing off into the distance, then he opened them and sat up.

"Morons," he said.

He rubbed the back of his neck then got to his feet. He was okay. A few aches and pains, which were going to feel a lot worse tomorrow, and some ringing in his ears, but nothing he couldn't handle. He picked up his bike and examined it closely. There was surprisingly little damage. One of the forks looked like it was out of alignment, but Chris would fix that up—his friend was really good with mechanical stuff. Better not to ride the bike until he'd had a look at it, though.

He wheeled it through the field, back along the narrow path and down the main road where the cars whizzed by far too quickly, until he was back in the town. As he reached Doherty's Shop, old Mrs. Doherty came running out to meet him. Running was pushing it a bit—it was more like she was speed-shuffling.

"Brian, Brian," she cried.

"Hi, Mrs. Doherty."

"Are you okay?"

"Me? I'm fine. What about you?"

"I wasn't the one who was chased by a couple of baloobas."

Brian wasn't sure what a balooba was, but he was fairly certain she wasn't using the term as a compliment. "Ah, that was nothing."

"Nothing? Nothing? You were a brave young man taking them on. And for my sake, too. You're a hero in my eyes. Now, come in here and tell me all about it."

Despite his protests, she brought him into her shop and made him sit on a little wooden stool while she peered over her large-framed glasses and attended to the cuts and scratches on his hands and face. As usual, the shop was empty. Brian couldn't understand why she even bothered opening most of the time. Newpark had three large supermarkets—and two smaller ones—where everyone went to do their shopping. Most of what Mrs. Doherty sold wasn't exactly what people bought anymore, either: hard candies, newspapers, and some homegrown vegetables. Brian had no idea how old she was, but his dad had once told him she was an old woman when he was Brian's age, so he reckoned she must be pretty ancient.

"That was very brave of you," she said again. "Brave, but foolish."

"I like being foolish," Brian said.

He had been passing by earlier when he'd seen gorillas one and two inside the shop, hassling Mrs. Doherty. They were getting cigarettes and drinks and chocolate and told her they had no cash on them, but that they'd come back and pay tomorrow. Brian knew that they had no intention of coming back and paying. And he didn't like the look of fear on Mrs. Doherty's face, either. So he'd grabbed a two-liter bottle of soda, shaken it up, and emptied it all over the bigger guy. He couldn't have much of a sense of humor because he'd taken it badly, which is why Brian ended up being chased by them. He might have ended up crashing his bike, but at least he'd gotten them off Mrs. Doherty's back.

"Next time you see someone causing trouble in my shop,

let me handle it. I don't want you getting hurt. After all, you have your whole life ahead of you. The majority of my life is made up of yesterdays."

"You're not *that* old," Brian said.

Mrs. Doherty smiled at that.

"Why didn't you call someone for help?" Brian asked.

"If I did, there'd be a fuss and my son would find out. He doesn't like me working here—he'd prefer me to be sitting safe at home staring at the walls. I keep the shop open so I don't have to do that. I know you might think it's quiet, but people often drop in for a chat. I like it that way."

She wouldn't let him leave without giving him some free groceries. Since his father never went shopping, he was glad to get them.

"They're just to say thank you," she said. "It's nice to know that some young people will step in and help when there's trouble around."

"Any time," Brian said, and he meant it.

"What in the name of all that's good and holy is that green thing?" Brian's father asked, snorting to express his disgust.

"It's kale," Brian said.

"Kale?" His father poked at it with his fork, before repeating the word. "Kale."

"It's a vegetable."

Brian's father, Patrick Duffy McDonnell, but known by most as Mucky, stared at his son.

"What have I told you about vegetables?"

"That you don't like them?"

"That I don't like them—do you hear him?" he asked, even though there was nobody else in the house other than Brian and himself. "I don't just not like them, I hate them. I haven't eaten a vegetable since 1983 and I have no intention of starting now."

It was quite possibly true that Mucky hadn't eaten a vegetable in over thirty years, unless you counted potatoes as a vegetable, which he didn't. Even when he got his welfare check and went to the diner, he never got mushy peas or onion rings or anything like that. Most of the time it was a burger and fries or sausage and fries. Pizza, if he was feeling fancy. But never a vegetable. If Brian's father ever had to become a vegetarian for medical reasons, he'd be dead by the end of the week.

Mucky shifted the green contents of his plate onto Brian's before digging into a large portion of chicken nuggets. "You can eat it. And make a better lunch tomorrow, right? Where did you get it from anyway?"

"Mrs. Doherty grows it herself and she threw it in with the groceries. She said we might like it. Thought we'd give it a try," Brian said. He hadn't told him the truth about what he'd been up to earlier and he wasn't going to tell him, either.

His father was looking at him strangely, as if something wasn't quite right.

"You been fighting?" he asked eventually.

Brian had been home for over an hour, yet it was only now that Mucky noticed his son was in much poorer physical condition than he'd been the last time he'd seen him, which, he thought, was either yesterday or the day before that.

"No, I fell off my bike."

"That's good. If you looked like that after a fight, it means you'd have lost. Don't want any son of mine embarrassing the family by taking a beating." He got up from the small kitchen table, took a packet of chocolate cookies from the cupboard, and slumped onto the couch. "Make me a cup of tea, like a good lad. And Sharon's coming over in a while, so tidy the place up a bit. You've left it in a real mess."

Mucky had never been the world's greatest father, but he hadn't always been like this, either. The biggest problem with Brian and Mucky was that they had nothing in common other than the ability to make smart remarks at the wrong time. People had always said Brian was like his mom and they were right. Mucky was interested in cars and football and playing cards, and Brian didn't like any of those things. They never had much to say to each other and it had always been a little awkward between them, but Brian's mom had a wonderful knack for making things all right. But then she left and now he only saw her every couple of months. Brian and his dad hadn't been the same since she'd gone—they just seemed to get on each other's nerves.

Brian's mom used to collect fridge magnets for some

reason, those ones that had inspirational quotes. They'd been stuck all over the fridge door, a couple of them falling off anytime someone went to fetch milk or butter. Brian remembered a bright orange one that was stuck right beside the handle. It read: *Your life does not get better by chance—it gets better by change.* The day after his mom had left, he'd thrown it in the trash. Anytime there had been changes in his life things had only gotten worse. *Yes,* he thought, *anyone who thinks change is good is an idiot.*

"I'm going to go out for a while, to meet the guys."

"Huh?" His father wasn't listening.

"Once I've tidied up, I'm going to go out for a while."

"What are you telling me for?" Mucky said.

Excerpt from travel book:

JOTTINGS FROM A SMALL IRELAND

by William Wrydaughter (2005)

The town of Newpark isn't new and it doesn't contain a park. And that is the most interesting fact about what has to be Ireland's dullest town. I had been having a wonderful time traveling around the Emerald Isle when one evening, while sitting by a roaring fire in a cozy country pub being stared at by a cheerful three-legged dog—who also happened to be called William—I told the men at the next table that I hadn't had a boring day since I'd set foot in the country. Instead of accepting what I thought of as a compliment, they took my statement as a challenge.

"Oh, there's some dull places here, all right. A lot more dull than you'd find in one of your fancier parts of the world," one of them said. "Baile Eilís, that place would drive you nearly mad with boredom. The dogs can't be bothered to bark and even the crows caw wearily."

"There's a place in the west called Carraig Cruach. I got so bored there once I started reading *Ulysses*," another said.

"Carraig Cruach is like New York compared to some of the towns I've worked in," said a hairy-faced man.

I sat back, slowly draining my creamy pint of stout from its glass as they argued among themselves for a while. Each tried to top the last with names of places known for their ability to suck the life from your bones, mentioning towns and villages so dull that, according to these men, visitors frequently fell into twenty-hour sleeps, while locals spent every evening crying in despair. Each new customer in the pub was more than happy to join in the game, offering stories of how crushingly dull a place was until an old man, who had been listening intently for almost half an hour, finally spoke up.

"Newpark," he said simply.

The others nodded their heads slowly in agreement, as if this was the final word on the matter. The man looked like Gandalf or Dumbledore, although his wise and wizardly demeanor was offset somewhat by the shiny blue anorak he was wearing.

"Newpark?" I asked with the innocence of someone who'd yet to encounter what I will loosely call its charms.

"Dullest place I've ever been," the old man said. "It's not unpretty, the people are pleasant, and it's a large enough town, so it tricks you into thinking something interesting might happen, but it never does. Nothing interesting ever happens there."

When I heard those words, I knew I had to see it. This was exactly the sort of low-key anti-adventure I usually enjoyed. I traveled to Newpark the next day. At first glance, it looked unremarkable. It was indeed a large town by Irish standards. It had pubs and restaurants and shops, but there was something about it, something I couldn't quite put my finger on. After a day, I realized the old man was right. It was hideously, unequivocally, gut-wrenchingly dull. And I like dullness. An open fire, a crossword, and a nice cup of tea are my idea of heaven, but Newpark . . . it stretched me to my boredom-loving limits. The only good thing that occurred in the two days I spent there was that I solved a centuries-old medical dilemma: I had finally found the cure for insomnia, and its name was Newpark.

THREE

"Nothing ever happens around here."

There were only two people in the neat and tidy yard, and they were brothers. Twins, actually, fraternal, not identical, though they did look similar—both had thick brown hair and large brown eyes. But they were very different in personality, almost as if they had been designed to be opposites.

Chris, the slightly older of the two, didn't look up from his mobile phone. He was in the middle of an adventure game that he'd been playing for most of the last forty-two hours.

If Chris had his way, everything would be quiet and peaceful most of the time. Peace and quiet were good, allowing him to play his games and read his books and think what he increasingly considered to be great thoughts. When Chris grew up, he wanted to be a game designer or a scientist or an engineer. The problem was a lot of the time he was stuck in a noisy environment where most of the noise was created by his younger—by twenty-nine minutes—brother, who didn't seem to have an *off* switch. To make matters worse, they had to share a bedroom.

"Nothing ever happens here," Sam repeated. "Newpark is so boring."

"I heard you the first time."

"You didn't say anything," Sam said.

"Because I was ignoring you," Chris said. "And you're wrong. Something does happen here. Something happens everywhere. The sun rises, people go to work. What you mean is nothing *you* find exciting ever happens here. Anyway, it's not like you have to put up with life around here for much longer."

"Why do you have to be such a pain?" Sam said. "And where's Hannah?"

The yard they were in, and the large stone-gray house that it surrounded, was the home of Hannah Fitzgerald, one of their best friends and a co-founder of the Misfits Club. They had been members, along with Brian McDonnell, since they were eight years old.

"Heads up, here's Brian," Sam said, spotting him coming down the narrow, tree-lined road that ended at Florence Parkinson's farm. The Fitzgeralds and Parkinsons were the only two homes at this end of a road that was a mile from Newpark town center. Florence Parkinson, who was either a charming or an eccentric lady, depending on your point of view, lived by herself. Since Hannah was an only child, the total population of the two houses was three adults and one child, meaning the cul-de-sac was usually a quiet place.

Chris didn't look up from his game.

"Looks like he's been attacked by a bear or something."

It still wasn't enough to make Chris look up.

"What happened?" Sam asked as Brian limped toward him, pushing his bike through the gate and onto the graveled path, which was bordered by a variety of expensive shrubs. Brian knew they were expensive because when he'd accidentally biked over some of them six months earlier, Hannah's mother had spent a good five minutes lecturing him about how much it would cost to replace the ones he'd destroyed.

"Fell off my bike," Brian said. He'd tell Sam about the chase later; he wasn't in the mood right now.

Sam took the bike from him and inspected it. "Well, it doesn't look too bad. Mostly surface stuff. I'll get Chris to check it out before we leave." He looked past Brian, across the road to the farmhouse that was owned by the old woman whose name he could never quite remember. Hannah was coming out of the house, accompanied by a girl around her own age. "Who's that with Hannah?" he asked.

The girl had long red hair and unlike Hannah, who was stomping her way through the muddy yard, the pale girl was picking her steps carefully, as if she was worried about getting even a single speck of dirt on her shoes.

"Maybe it's one of her cousins," Brian said.

Hannah had a lot of cousins, but none of them looked like her because she'd been adopted from Vietnam when she was a baby and all her cousins had been born in Ireland.

"Nah, don't think so. She looks like she's our age. Hannah's only cousin our age is that weirdo with the snotty nose. You know, the guy who eats what he picks when he thinks no one's looking."

"Oh, him. He *is* a weirdo," Brian agreed.

"Hey, guys," Hannah said as she hopped over the wall.

The red-haired girl chose the more traditional route of going through the gate.

"Hey, Hannah," Sam said. "Who's that with you?"

Sam wasn't the sort of person who had the patience to wait around for polite introductions.

"This is Amelia."

"Hello," Amelia said.

"Great to meet you. You can call me Sam. Mainly 'cause that's my name."

He slapped her on the shoulder a little too enthusiastically. She almost toppled over.

"Sorry about that," he said.

"That guy who's too rude to look up from his phone is Chris. He's Sam's brother," Hannah said.

"Not too rude. Just finishing a game."

"Take no notice of him," Hannah said.

Amelia smiled, although she didn't feel like smiling.

"We're the Misfits Club, by the way," Sam said. "Me, Hannah, my brother Chris—that's the guy who says he isn't rude—and Brian is the battered-looking guy." Sam gestured to his friend standing to his right.

"Hey," Brian said.

"Hello," Amelia replied.

"We started the club when we were really young," Sam explained. "You know, for adventures and stuff. It's kind of stupid."

"It's not stupid," Brian said, his cheeks reddening. He hated it when anyone called it stupid. Really hated it.

"He kind of likes this club," Hannah said.

"I got that," Amelia said. "So, what do you do?"

"Hang out, mostly. Chat, play games, stuff like that. We're going to the movies tomorrow."

"I see."

Not, *that sounds great* or *I think that's cool*, Brian thought, but *I see*, as if she found the whole thing beneath her. He was almost certain that her lip curled a little when she said it, as if she was sneering at them. He had only just met her, but he was already taking a dislike to this girl.

"The Misfits Club isn't just a club—it's a state of mind," Chris said.

"But it is an actual club, too, right?" Amelia said.

"Yes, it's a cl—"

"Come on," Hannah said to Amelia. "I'll show you our headquarters."

This is the den. It's where we have our meetings," Hannah said.

The den was a large wooden shed. There were two sheds in the yard: One was for all the gardening equipment; the other, the slightly shabbier of the two, had served as the headquarters of the Misfits Club for almost four years. It was as cozy as a warm hug on a cold night. Beanbags sat on a large old rug that crept to the walls of the shed. A small bookshelf filled with Hannah's favorite mystery stories was placed beneath the only window and the walls were covered in film posters she'd gotten from the local movie theater.

"It's really nice," Amelia said as she glanced around, checking for spiders and any other bugs that might be lying in wait for her.

"You here on vacation, Amelia?" Chris asked. He leaped on a beanbag and burrowed his way in until he was comfortable.

"I'm here to visit my grandmother," Amelia replied, a little cagily. "I'm going to look after her for a few weeks. She, er, needs a bit of taking care of."

"You can sit down if you like," Hannah said.

Amelia looked unsure. The others had settled into their beanbags, leaving the two girls standing.

Before she'd decided whether to sit or continue looking awkward and uncomfortable, she heard the click-clacking of Mrs. Fitzgerald's shoes on the paving stones outside the shed. The door swung open to reveal a round-faced woman who looked extremely jolly. *Jolly* was not the right word to describe either Mr. or Mrs. Fitzgerald, not when you could choose words like *practical* or *serious* or *joyless*. They may not have had much in the way of a sense of humor, but they were good parents and Hannah never wanted for anything, other than a sense of freedom—they were constantly monitoring her comings and goings and always fretting that something bad was going to happen to her.

Mrs. F carried in a tray of goodies—crusty sandwich rolls, freshly baked cakes, and homemade lemonade. Brian's eyes lit up. Even though he'd just had lunch, he was always hungry.

"You must be Amelia. How lovely to finally meet you in person rather than just seeing you through a car window as your father drives by."

"Hello, Mrs. Fitzgerald. Nice to meet you, too."

"What lovely manners," Mrs. Fitzgerald said. She was impressed by things like politeness and good manners yet, for some reason Sam failed to understand, distinctly unimpressed by things like his ability to belch the first nine letters of the alphabet without drawing breath.

"Mom, we're having a club meeting," Hannah said.

"That's her way of telling me to get lost," Mrs. Fitzgerald said to Amelia.

"Is it okay to use your bathroom? I'd like to wash my hands before I eat," Amelia said.

"Of course. Follow me," Mrs. Fitzgerald said.

"She's a barrel of laughs, isn't she?" Brian said as soon as Amelia had left.

"Give her a break," Hannah said. "She's only just met us. It's not easy meeting new people."

"Why did you bring her here, Hannah? She's like, I don't know, Miss Fancypants or something. Washing her hands and being polite and making conversation with your mother. It's not natural."

"You just don't want her joining the club," Chris said.

"She's joining the club?" Brian asked incredulously.

"Yeah, why not? The more, the merrier," Sam said.

"And it'll be nice to have another girl around," Hannah said.

"Wait a second—I didn't agree to that. I don't want her joining the club when she could be, you know, all Goldilocksy and stuff. It's just been the four of us for years. Why do you want to change it now?"

"Come on, Brian, what difference does it make?" Hannah asked. "It's not like we're going to be together for much longer anyway."

At the end of August, just over two weeks from now, Sam, Chris, and the rest of their family—three brothers, two sisters, two parents, an elderly cat, and a dog with a serious peeing problem—were moving to Galway. Their mother had been offered a place at the university to study medicine even though she was in her forties, and, since their father spent a lot of time working in Galway as it was, it made sense to move. It didn't make much sense to Brian, though, who seemed to be more upset at the thought of his friends moving than they were.

"And what do we do these days except hang around and eat and laugh at the stupid body noises Sam makes?" Hannah continued.

"They're not stupid. Some cultures would consider what I do to be verging on musical genius," Sam muttered. "Even orchestras have wind instruments."

"Not that kind of wind," Chris said.

"We do more than hang around," Brian said. "We investigate and we have adventures. Amelia won't have a clue what to do if we get caught up in—"

"When was our last real adventure?" Hannah asked.

"We've had tons of them. It's hard to remember them all, there's been so many. That one, you know, when we did, with the . . . This isn't a memory test, you know."

"If you can remember any really exciting adventure we've had in the last year before Amelia gets back, then I promise you I won't ask her to join."

"Deal. Now, everyone be quiet while I try to think," Brian said.

He was still trying to remember when Amelia arrived back in the shed a few minutes later. They dug into the food and chatted a little awkwardly in the way people who are getting to know each other sometimes do before Hannah got to the point.

"Would you like to join our club?" she asked. "I know it's a bit cheesy—"

Brian rolled his eyes.

"—but we'd love it if you did. Wouldn't we, guys?"

"Definitely," Chris said.

Sam gave the thumbs-up as he grabbed another sandwich. Brian didn't show any encouragement, but he didn't disagree, either, at least not out loud.

"Great, I'd really like that," Amelia said.

"If she's going to join, she has to pass the test," Brian said.

"Test? What test?" Amelia asked.

"It's nothing bad," Hannah said. "Just a game we invented when we formed the club. Anyone who wants to join has to play one round to see if they've got what it takes to be a Misfit."

"If you find social situations really awkward or you spend more time reading books than people think is healthy or when you make a choice it *always* turns out to be the wrong one, then you've already got what it takes," Sam said.

"The game's called Gravest Danger," Brian said, ignoring Sam.

Chris was quick to reassure Amelia. "Don't worry, it's not as bad as it sounds," he said.

"Only two people have ever died while playing it," Sam said.

SOME DOS AND DON'TS OF GRAVEST DANGER

by Hannah Fitzgerald

DON'TS:

1. Don't leave the plug in the bathtub and then leave the faucet running until all the water flows over the side of the tub and runs down the stairs. You might think it would make a "stairs waterfall" and be brilliant for the white-water-rafting segment of the game, but it only makes the carpet soggy and parents go absolutely stark raving mad (and not in a funny way).

2. If one of the players gets taken by a vampire during the game and is killed, then they shouldn't lie dead in the hall covered in ketchup blood as this tends to freak out any passing grandmother with poor eyesight and may cause her to faint, which only leads to more shouting from parents.

3. Clues from the detective section of the game should not be tied to the collar of an aggressive dog. Stitches and tetanus shots hurt.

4. Bike wheelies are fun, but can lead to broken arms, which really slow down the game. No bike wheelies from now on.

<u>DOS:</u>

1. Do wear protective clothing, especially gloves, if handling anything hot, even if somebody (Sam) tells you it's not hot because that somebody (still Sam) thinks it's fun to see someone roll around on the ground in pain. It's not fun. It's mean and painful, and apologizing later doesn't mean you're going to be forgiven. (Got it, Sam?)
2. Remember that permanent marker is actually permanent. That means it won't come off the walls, so large drawings on the living room wall are not a good idea.
3. Have fun.

FOUR

"Ignore him," Hannah said to Amelia. "He's only joking. It's just a board game. Nobody's ever died."

"*Yet*," Sam said, easing himself out of the beanbag.

"See what I have to put up with? I don't know how I've managed to stay so sane," Chris said.

"Okay, to play Gravest Danger we have to go into the house. We need a bit more room than we have here in headquarters," Hannah said.

"I thought it was a board game," Amelia said.

"It is, but it can get a little action-y," Sam said.

The interior of the Fitzgerald house was nice. Too nice for Brian's liking. It was as perfect as a show house and everything Hannah's parents owned looked expensive and breakable. Every time he came over, he always worried that he was the one who'd accidentally do the breaking. Her parents were a bit frosty with him anyway, mainly because they didn't like his dad, he suspected, and the last thing he wanted was to give them a reason to ban him from the house. Brian much preferred the shed. He could relax there.

Hannah led them into what had once been her playroom. There were two couches and a low wooden table in between them. A television attached to a top-of-the-line game console hung on the wall. Sam crossed the room and opened a cupboard filled with old books and board games. All the games from their childhood were there—Monopoly, Clue, Stratego—but Hannah pulled out a battered old shoe box covered with brown paper and held together by yellowed bits of Scotch tape.

Chris's face lit up. "I haven't seen that in such a long time."

Amelia wasn't sure what was supposed to be exciting about it. It just looked like an ordinary shoe box to her, yet Chris was staring at it like he'd just discovered a long-lost relic from his youth.

"Everybody who joins the club has to play one round of this game," Hannah said, opening the shoe box.

Amelia peered inside. There were some dice and some figurines—a silver knight, some kind of scuffed Star Wars character, a ferocious-looking dragon, and a boy and a girl. Hannah took out the girl figurine and handed it to Amelia.

"That's going to be you," she said, taking the Star Wars character for herself. "This one's a bounty hunter."

"*Not the boy!*" Chris and Sam shouted at the same time.

"Ah no, I have to be the boy? He's the worst. Can't I be the dragon? It's much cooler," Brian said.

"Sorry, buddy," Sam said, grabbing the dragon. "You snooze, you lose."

Hannah took out the folded board, which had been made by attaching four old cereal boxes together. The tape that joined them was yellow and brittle in places. A hand-drawn path, numbered from one to a hundred, snaked around the board. Occasionally, the numbers were broken up by little labeled drawings. The labels had names like *Pit of Fire*, *Memory Puzzle*, or *Undead Attack*. Hannah removed a pile of cards that had also been cut out from cereal boxes. A piece of white paper with handwriting upon it had been glued to each one of the cards. Hannah took the cards, turned them upside down, and placed them in the center of the board.

Amelia saw the words written on the back of the card at the top of the pile: *Ultimate Test*. She was intrigued.

"I definitely have to play a game of Gravest Danger to join the club?" she asked.

Four heads nodded their agreement. "Do I have to win?"

"No. The game is a test of character. It's just to see if you're up for adventures. If you don't like the game, then you won't like being part of the club," Chris said.

"So, you have lots of adventures?"

"Um, yeah, we'll talk about that in a while. We'd better get started. Sam and me have to get back home in a couple of hours. Our mom's making us have a family night."

"Yes, we really are a wild bunch, aren't we?" Sam said.

Brian wasn't saying much, but his mood had improved. He was surprised at the anticipation he felt about playing the game. They hadn't played Gravest Danger in a long time. He couldn't remember why. Now that they were about to begin, he realized how much he used to enjoy it, although what he'd liked most of all was the time they'd spent designing it. He remembered the laughs they'd had when they were coming up with the rules—sitting on the floor in the cramped playroom in Hannah's old house, the rain pounding on the windows, drawings, sketches, and half-written rules all around them on the carpet. They'd spent more time telling each other jokes than they had making the game.

"Okay, Amelia, the rules are fairly simple," Hannah began. "You have to get around the board from start to finish without being caught by the rest of us. We're the hunters, you're the hunted. You get two rolls first to get a head start. Along the way, you might land on some squares like Pit of Fire and so on. Then you have to draw an Ultimate Test card and face whatever danger or test is written on the card. Got it?"

"Seems fairly straightforward."

"Great, then let's begin."

Amelia took the die in her hand, shook it around for longer than was helpful, long enough for Sam to blow out his cheeks in frustration, then rolled it far too vigorously.

It rattled its way across the table, along the carpet, and under the couch.

"Sorry," Amelia said.

"Nothing to worry about," Sam replied. He got to his feet and lifted the couch at one end until there was enough of a gap for someone to reach in. He grunted with the exertion. The couch was heavier than it looked. "I can't hold this forever. Help me out, SpongeBrian SquareHead."

"Oh, right," Brian said. He grabbed the die, pausing to check the number in the face. "You rolled a four, Amelia."

"Good solid start," Sam said, letting the couch down more violently than he intended.

"Okay, now roll again," Chris said.

Amelia rolled a three this time and moved forward to the seventh square.

"Nice one. You can't get caught this time. Six is the most anyone can roll in one go and you're on square seven, so you're safe," Sam said.

"I think she understands how dice work," Hannah said.

"Just trying to be helpful."

"Funny and interesting thing—since we're only using one of them, then it's *die*. When you're using two or more they're called *dice*," Chris said.

"You really don't understand what the words *funny* or *interesting* mean, do you?" Sam said, rolling his eyes.

Amelia managed to stay ahead of the hunters for the

next few moves before she landed on her first Ultimate Test square.

"Go ahead, pick up the card. There's nothing to worry about," Hannah said.

"Or is there?" Brian said in a creepy voice.

Amelia tentatively reached over and picked up one of the cards lying in the center of the board. She read it and looked puzzled.

"It says *Ten-second Monster Avoidance Challenge*," she said.

"Oh, that's not a bad one," Chris said. "Three of us pretend we're monsters and . . . wow, that sounds really weak when I say it out loud. What age were we when we wrote this game?"

"Don't dis the game. The game is fine. One of us times it, usually Chris, and you have to avoid being tagged by the rest of us for ten seconds. It might sound easy, but the room's small, so—"

"I have to avoid three of you in this room?"

"Yep. You get tagged by a monster, you lose and you freeze in the game for a turn. Good chance we'll catch up with you then."

"And if I avoid you for ten seconds, I move on in the game?"

"That's it."

Amelia looked around the room. Two couches and a table were the only hiding places, but with three people after you it didn't look like she'd be able to avoid them for long. Ten seconds might not seem like long, but it'd feel like it was forever in this small space.

"You okay for timing, Chris?" Hannah asked.

"Yep, I'm on it."

He had his mobile phone already set to stopwatch mode. Hannah, Sam, and Brian gathered by the door in one corner of the room, while Amelia went to the other corner. She took a few deep breaths, then bounced up and down on her toes, trying to get some energy into her limbs.

"Everyone ready?"

"Yes," Hannah and Brian said.

Sam growled, getting into character. Half measures meant less than half the fun, as far as he was concerned, and with games like this, it was always more fun to give it your all.

"Right, then," Chris said. "Monsters attack."

They raced forward in unison at first, then they split as they had to edge around the table and couch. Amelia stood in the corner, still bouncing on her toes, making no effort to move out of the way. Brian hesitated for a moment, wondering what her plan was, as the others rushed forward— Sam baring his teeth, his hands shaped into claws—and were within touching distance immediately.

Was that a tear in her eye? She looked afraid. Amelia dropped to her haunches and covered her head with her hands. Her shoulders shook, as if she was sobbing.

They stopped and looked at each other, unsure of what to do. The two boys indicated to Hannah that she should be the one to say something.

"Amelia, it's okay. There's no need to be scared. It's only a game. We're not really going to hurt you."

When Amelia spoke, her voice was muffled by her arms, but still shaky. "Are you sure?"

"Absolutely."

"Chris, are the ten seconds up?" Amelia asked.

"Yeah, why?"

Amelia got to her feet. She wasn't crying, not even a little bit. "Guess I win, then."

"No way—" Sam began.

"Wait a second, you were pretending?" Brian asked. He couldn't process what had happened. "But that's cheating."

"Are you sure?" Amelia asked. "I don't remember you saying that before we started."

"I didn't say, but it, well, it was understood, right? Hannah, Chris, you're the rule experts. That's not right, is it?"

"She wins. Her move was sneaky, but effective."

They're right, Brian thought. It *was* sneaky. Just like he'd been sneaky when he'd pretended to be unconscious in the field after being chased by the two gorillas. Maybe Amelia wasn't as much of a drip as he'd thought.

"Nice one, Amelia," Sam said. "Your way was much easier than when I last tried to avoid the monsters. I jumped over the couch and cracked my coccyx on the corner of the table. Had to go to the doctor. It was touch and go as to whether I'd have to have surgery or not. In the end, I had to wear a cast on my butt for six weeks."

Amelia wasn't sure how to reply to that, so she said nothing.

"Almost none of that is true," Hannah whispered to her.

The next few rounds of Gravest Danger flew by and Amelia managed to stay ahead of the hunters until the final stretch. She had to do a thirty-second headstand, give a short speech on her favorite mythical creature, find objects hidden in the room from a series of two-word clues, figure out who had killed Sam in a locked-room murder-mystery game, and make a complete circuit of the outside of the house without touching the ground. This last task led her to walk across windowsills and wheeled bins and she almost pulled a plastic drainpipe from the wall, struggling for balance.

After an exhausting, yet exhilarating, hour and thirty-seven minutes, the game was almost over. Amelia was four spaces ahead of Hannah, the nearest hunter, and had dispatched Brian and Sam back to square one by accurately reciting an old, seventeenth-century witch's spell backward that she'd memorized immediately after the monster-hunting section. Chris had been just behind her for most of the game, but had begun to flag when he'd lost his balance and fallen into a fiery pit.

"So, if I roll a two or above, I'll be safe," Amelia said.

"Yep, you'll have reached the final square and the hunters can't catch you."

Amelia shook the die in her hand, blew on it for luck, whispered something to herself, and rolled it.

A four.

She'd done it. She leaped in the air, far more excited at her victory than she'd expected. The others didn't look pleased, though, and nobody was congratulating her.

"Have I done something wrong?" she asked.

"No, of course not. It's just that you're not quite finished yet."

Amelia's brow wrinkled in confusion.

"You have to pick up one final Ultimate Test card," Chris said.

"Oh, okay. Sure."

The Ultimate Tests had been a bit quirky, but she hadn't found them too difficult, either. She picked up the card on top of the pile. All it said was: *The Cabin in the Woods*. That wasn't very clear. She handed the card to Hannah.

"What does it say?" Brian asked.

Hannah turned the card around so they could all read it.

"No way," Sam said.

"What does it mean?" Amelia asked.

Sam turned to her. "Well, Amelia, how do you feel about poltergeists?"

THE NEWPARK ECHO

Thursday, December 20, 1979

GHOST IN THE WOODS—LOCAL WOMAN SHOCKED

A local woman received a terrible shock while walking her dog last Tuesday morning. Dolores McDougal (51), originally from Lough, but living in Newpark for the past twenty-three years, was taking her dog, Dexter, for a stroll in Micawber Woods at 7 a.m. when she got the fright of her life.

"I was up early because I was going to take the children Christmas shopping. Pat, my husband, normally takes the dog for a walk, but he was feeling a bit rough after his work Christmas party, so I said I'd take him myself. To be honest, I was glad to get out of the house because things are a bit crazy around there at Christmas, especially when the boys drink red lemonade for breakfast. It makes them far too excitable."

Shortly after leaving the house, Dolores had reached the edge of the woods, when Dexter unexpectedly took off in pursuit of what Dolores described as either a large squirrel or a small badger. After almost fifteen minutes, she found the dog cowering by a derelict cottage deep in the woods.

"I thought the dog was upset because he knew I'd

be mad with him for running off. Next thing I know, this ghostly apparition is coming right at me. It materialized out of nowhere. There was this green glow coming off it and it had the most horrible face I've ever seen. I've never been more frightened in my life. It shot straight at me and I ran away as fast as I could. I didn't stop running until I got home. I haven't been right since."

The cottage was once the property of Patrick Grenham, a hermit who lived there with his dog in the early part of the century. It is reputed that Grenham got lost in the woods looking for his pet on a winter's night and died in the cold weather. The rumors are that his ghost wanders the woods constantly, searching for his lost companion. He has been spotted on numerous occasions since his death, but this was the first sighting in a number of years.

"When my husband saw me, he told me I looked like I'd seen a ghost," Dolores said. "He thought it was really funny that that's what he said when I told him shortly afterward what had really happened, but I don't think it was funny at all."

Luckily, Dexter the dog turned up safe and sound later that day, but Dolores won't be venturing into the dark woods anytime soon.

"Not if I live to be a hundred will I ever go in there again," she said. "And I'll be warning everyone else to stay away as well."

FIVE

"So, are you ready?" Hannah asked.

"Ready?" It dawned on Amelia what she was being asked. "You want to go now?"

"Gravest Danger doesn't finish until you've completed the last test," Chris said, while checking something on his mobile phone. "But we'll have to hurry up—Sam and I have to get home soon."

Amelia did her best to hide her panic at what lay ahead. "It's okay, you know," Brian said. "You don't have to do it if you're scared."

"Who said I was scared? Course I'm going to do it . . . Right, let's go, then," she said.

"That's the spirit," Sam said. He was thrilled to be doing something. He really didn't like just sitting around all the time.

The woods weren't far away and the easiest way to access them was by crossing the fields at the bottom of Hannah's yard. She'd told her mother that they were going for a walk and that they'd be back in an hour, so it wasn't as if they were heading off on some far-flung trek. Amelia picked her way around some cow dung, wondering if she would ever get used to the smell of the countryside.

They climbed a gate at the end of the first field, then squeezed through a gap at the bottom of the second until they reached a third, one where a flock of sheep was spread out, munching grass.

"They're not going to attack, are they?" Amelia asked.

"No, you're safe enough. Sheep attacks are rare events," Chris said.

"Did I tell you about my prank last night?" Sam asked.

Hannah and Brian groaned. "Please tell me it's not more Trick Whittington," Hannah said.

"What's Trick Whittington?" Amelia asked.

"My brother likes playing childish pranks on people, you know, the usual ones—salt in the sugar bowl, plastic wrap over the toilet seat. Last night, he woke me up at about two in the morning, dressed as a zombie—"

"It really freaked him out. He ran down the hallway screaming, waking up everyone in the house, and then he slammed into the bathroom door and almost broke his nose. I never laughed so much in all my life," Sam said, smiling at the memory. "There were tears rolling down my cheeks and everything."

"Yep, absolute terror followed by physical injury. Just a typical night at home," Chris said.

"I got Adeyinka to do the zombie makeup before she went to bed," Sam continued. "Took nearly two hours with all the caked blood and everything, and then I had to stay awake for another few hours to make sure Chris was in a deep sleep, but it was totally worth it."

"When he does stuff like that, he says he's not really responsible, that it's some kind of mysterious alter ego playing the pranks, someone he likes to call Trick Whittington after Dick Whittington in the old fairy tale," Chris said.

"I really don't know what to say to that," Amelia said.

"There's nothing to say," Hannah said. "Sure you still want to join the club?"

The final field was steeply banked, which made it difficult to traverse. At the end of the sloping greenery lay the forest, dark and unwelcoming.

"The cabin is in there?" Amelia asked, hoping that someone would contradict her.

"Technically, it's a cottage, not a cabin. We call it *Cabin in the Woods* in the game because it sounds cooler."

Without warning, Sam set off down the slope, running as fast as he could, his legs almost a blur.

"He's going to fall," Hannah said. She said it wearily, like she'd seen this sort of behavior from him a hundred times before.

And, right on cue, he did fall. He stumbled for a moment, windmilling his arms to try to regain his balance, but his momentum was too great and he went head over heels, then tumbled sideways, his body bouncing around, before he rolled to a stop at the edge of the forest. He was hidden by the thick, untamed grass.

He popped up suddenly, a big fake smile plastered on his face, trying to look perfectly normal.

"I'm okay," he shouted, but when he started walking again he appeared to be trying to disguise a limp.

"Why would anyone build a house out here? It's so far from anywhere," Amelia said.

"Newpark didn't exist when the cottage was first built. There was a road here once, but it hasn't been used in a long, long time. It's all covered over with moss and weeds and earth now," Chris said.

"It's not too late to back out, you know," Hannah said. "It's only a game."

"No, no, I don't want to back out. I'm looking forward to this," Amelia lied.

They followed Sam's path down the slope until they reached the edge of the forest. They could hear the gurgling of a stream just beyond the brambles that barred their path. Sam and Brian and Hannah stamped them down until their way was clear.

Once they stepped inside the forest, Amelia felt a coldness grip her spine as the daylight fell away. She looked back to reassure herself that the world was still there and of course it was. There was the sloping field and the sun in the sky and, reassuringly, Hannah and Brian, and Sam and Chris.

"Okay, let's go," Brian said, striding purposefully forward.

"This poltergeist," Amelia began, broaching the subject gently as she carefully picked her way along the forest path—even when terrified she was determined not to scuff her good shoes—"you don't really believe in it, do you?"

"Lots of people have seen it over the years," Brian said, thrashing at a stray thorn branch with a stick he'd picked up. "None of them have ever gone back in the woods again and they've sworn they never will."

Amelia gulped.

"I don't believe in it. It's ridiculous," Chris said. "Let's look at it logically. First of all—"

"He always tries to ruin everything with facts and logic," Brian grumbled.

"Hey, don't worry about it, Amelia. You'll be fine," Sam said. "At least there's no other dangerous creatures in the forest. If we were in Africa, we could be getting mauled by a tiger right now."

"No, we couldn't," Chris said. "There are no tigers in Africa."

"Of course there are. Where else would they be hanging around? Dublin?" Brian said.

"Come on, Brian. You know Chris watches all those David Attenborough programs. What's the point in arguing with him?" Sam said.

It took them another ten minutes to reach the cottage. It was built from stone and it was surprisingly intact. The windows weren't broken; the roof wasn't full of holes. There were streaks of black on the whitewash and what may once have been a garden had grown wild. Weeds crept and wound their way around the bottom of the stonework, but not the front door itself.

"That's weird," Chris said.

"What?" Brian asked.

"The weeds at the front door—"

"Hey, guys," Hannah interrupted, "don't mean to rush you or anything, but you've got that family night and my mom wants me back by seven. If I'm late, you know what happens."

"Grounded for days," Brian, Chris, and Sam said in unison.

"For being late? Why are they so strict?" Amelia asked.

"Because Hannah was crazy when she was young and kept giving them heart attacks by doing all kinds of stuff," Sam said.

"What kind of stuff?"

"She once released the handbrake on the car and crashed it into a wall," Chris said. "Another time she brought home a stray Rottweiler she said was her new best friend and it ate half the couch."

"And she accidentally paid for a holiday to the Arctic online. Cost them thousands of euro," Brian said.

"She climbed on the roof of the house while they were in the garden. They were terrified she was going to fall off," Sam said.

"I wasn't going to fall. I'm an excellent climber," Hannah said.

"I think that was the one that sent them over the edge. Her mother hasn't been the same since and her dad started going gray after that," Chris said.

"So now they watch her like a hawk the whole time. It's kind of funny," Sam said.

"It's not funny. It's really annoying. I have to be sneaky or else I don't get to do anything that's fun," Hannah said. "I don't want to talk about them anymore."

"So what now?" Amelia asked.

"Now you go in," Hannah said.

Somehow, Amelia had known she was going to say that.

"You're not going to lock the door once I've gone inside?" Amelia asked.

"No way," Chris said. "That'd be cruel."

"It'd be funny, though," Sam said. He waved his arms around and spoke in a girlish voice. "Aarrgh, I'm trapped in here with a murderous ghost. Aaaaargggh."

When Hannah scowled at him, he decided it might not be that funny after all.

Hannah explained to Amelia what her two Gravest Danger tasks were: She had to spend a full five minutes in the cottage and take a selfie in front of the old stone fireplace in the living room. That was it. Once she'd left the cottage having done both those things, she'd be a fully fledged member of the Misfits Club, whether she liked it or not.

"Five minutes, right? I can manage that easily."

"That's the spirit," Hannah said.

She held up her hand for a high five. Amelia gently patted it, then, when Hannah wasn't looking, wiped her hand clean on a tissue.

The thought of going into the cottage made her queasy. There could be anything in there—fat juicy spiders, mice, giant rats. She felt her resolve draining away. Ghosts or poltergeists might end up being the least of her worries.

"If you panic and want to get out of there, then shout," Brian said.

"I won't panic," she said firmly.

She pushed through the front door. It creaked open. Some of the wood was rotting and looked as if it would crumble to the touch.

"Good luck," Hannah said. Amelia stepped inside and pulled the door shut behind her.

And then Amelia was alone.

Almost immediately, she heard a noise. It turned out to be her own panicked breathing. Before she took another step, she started the countdown timer on her phone. Even though Chris had said he'd time it, she wanted to know how long she had left.

All she had to do was find the fireplace, take the photograph, then get back to the front door, wait for the knock, and it would all be over.

The odor in the house was moldy, an unpleasant

woody dampness. The light from her phone flitted along the old stone walls, sending the darkness scurrying to the corners.

There were only three rooms in the cottage and to Amelia's relief she was able to find the living room immediately. It was filled with discarded furniture and clumps of grass grew through cracks in the concrete floor. If Amelia had been less nervous, she might have noticed that although the sofa in the center of the living room wasn't brand new, neither was it from the early 1900s.

"Do you think she's scared?" Hannah asked, squinting through a window.

Although she'd only known Amelia for a couple of hours, she felt strangely protective of her.

"It's not that scary in there," Brian said.

"If you don't believe in ghosts," Hannah said. "But what if you do?"

"Where are you going?" Chris asked.

Hannah reached for the door. "I'm not leaving her in there if she's scared. It's not right."

She pulled at the handle, but the door didn't open. It was stuck. It must have jammed when Amelia pulled it closed behind her.

Amelia nearly jumped out of her skin when she heard the door handle jiggling.

"The door's a bit stuck, but there's no need to worry," Hannah shouted.

"You nearly gave me a heart attack," Amelia replied.

"If you want to come out, let us know and we'll get the door open," Chris said.

"Fine, but stay quiet for now. The poltergeist is hardly likely to turn up if you're all chatting outside like a bunch of old people in a coffee shop."

"She's bossy," Brian said. "That's just what this club needs—someone bossing us around."

There was an air of sadness in the living room. Amelia couldn't pinpoint the reason why, but it was there, like morning mist on a river. She glanced at her phone to check the countdown timer, forgetting about the light from the phone's flashlight until she'd shone it directly into her own eyes, blinding herself for a moment.

"Oh, for goodness' sake," she said, rubbing her eyelids with her free hand. "What's wrong with me? I get an A on every exam and I nearly burn my own eyeballs."

She turned the phone at an angle so she could read the screen. Three minutes and sixteen seconds left. All she had to do was to walk to the fireplace and take a selfie. If she could get her legs to move. Why wouldn't they move?

Because she knew that the poltergeist was right behind her.

SIX

She spun around, her heart pounding so much she felt like it would burst out of her chest. But there was nothing there. Nothing at all.

It had just been her imagination—of course there was no poltergeist.

Breathing a huge sigh of relief, she focused on what was real—the small window to the left of the fireplace—crisscrossed with thin wooden slats. Outside in the forest, all was dark. She took another step forward.

And another.

Before she knew it, she was by the fireplace. It was time to take the photograph. She remembered to switch off the flashlight setting this time. She didn't like the sudden darkness.

"T-take the photo, Amelia," she said. The words stuttered from her mouth.

She found the camera icon and switched to selfie mode, the ghostly dark outline of her own face on the screen shocking her for a moment. She held it up, faked a smile, and pressed the button.

The flash popped. She had planned to take two or three pictures, but the moment the light flashed, she heard the wail. Then . . .

DUMPH!

Something outside the cottage thudded against the wall behind her.

Amelia didn't wait to find out what it was.

She ran.

And fell over the couch, landing on the ground in a mixture of dirt and dust. Cobwebs tangled in her hair. She flapped at them, then wiped a hand over her face, making sure there was nothing on her—no creatures, no poltergeists.

Amelia heard a little girl scream. She stopped dead, too afraid to move.

It took a moment before she realized she was the one who'd let out the scream. She scrambled to her feet, and somehow made it through the doorway and into the hall. She slammed up against the front door and thumped on it.

"Let me out, let me out."

The Misfits were on the other side, strung out in single file, one behind the other, involved in a tug-of-war with the door.

It opened and Amelia fell forward against Brian, starting a domino effect. One by one they all toppled onto the ground.

Hannah was the first one up. She grabbed Amelia's hand.

"Run," Hannah said.

Amelia didn't need to be told twice.

"I don't want to die," Chris screeched.

Nobody looked behind to see who or what was after them. Nobody wasted time checking. Nobody wanted to see what it was, or what it might be, or what form it might take. They just ran and tripped and bumped against each other and ran again, racing through the forest until they could see the sun and the fields ahead of them and they were free of the darkness.

Even as they emerged back into the real world, they kept running until they were half a mile beyond the forest's edge and they all collapsed into a quivering, exhausted heap.

"So, no such thing as poltergeists, huh?" Sam said when he'd recovered enough to speak.

Amelia's hands were trembling and her mouth was dust-dry. When she glanced across at Hannah she saw that even though she had turned as pale as any poltergeist, she also had a huge grin slapped on her face. Surely, she couldn't have enjoyed the terror?

"Who said it was a poltergeist?" Brian asked, sweat drenching the back of his head.

He hauled Hannah to her feet.

"Well, if it wasn't a poltergeist, why were we running?" she asked, her words all tumbling together with excitement.

"I ran because Amelia came out of there screaming her head off about a ghost," Sam said, "but I do feel kind of cowardly about it now."

"I didn't scream my head off," Amelia snapped.

Her natural politeness had been pushed to one side by her recent experiences.

"You were babbling on about a ghost or something and then when the door opened you pushed through us," Brian said.

Amelia glared at him. "Well, Mr. Brave Guy, why didn't you go in and investigate, then? Why did you run?"

"I—I—I—"

Much to his own annoyance, Brian didn't have an answer to that question. He'd run because Hannah had. It was an automatic reaction, but, just like Sam, he wasn't proud of it.

"Sorry about tripping you," Chris said to Sam.

Chris had panicked and grabbed on to Sam's leg as his brother was in the process of sprinting off, sending him tumbling to the ground. Instead of helping him up, Chris had taken the opportunity to race ahead of his more sporty sibling. He felt guilty about it now.

"No problem," Sam said. He knew Chris wasn't the bravest guy in the world. When he was younger he'd once had to hide behind the couch after being frightened by an episode of *The Fairly OddParents*.

"And sinking my teeth into your leg, that was a panicked reaction. I'm sorry about that, too."

"These things happen."

"Why were you in such a rush to get out of there, Amelia?" Hannah said.

"Because I saw something," Amelia replied.

"Wait a second," Chris said, suddenly interested. "You actually saw something?"

"Yes. Well, no. Maybe. I don't know. I heard something, though. A ghostly sound."

"What kind of ghostly sound?"

"A wailing," Amelia said.

"Ghosts wail, all right, so her story checks out," Sam said. "Like cows moo, dogs bark. Ghosts definitely wail."

"Ah, rats," Hannah said, glancing at the time on her phone. "I'm going to be late. Let's pick this up at my house."

"We have to go home as well," Chris said. In all the excitement, he'd almost forgotten about the family night. "We'll have to wait until tomorrow."

"Wait a second. We've just had an encounter with a ghost and we're going home like it's a normal day? That's crazy. We've got a lot to discuss," Sam said.

"Absolutely," Brian agreed. "This is the best thing that's happened to us in forever. We can't just do nothing."

"We've arranged to go to the movies tomorrow. It'll be the perfect cover for us to talk about all of this without my pesky parents meddling in our business. For some reason, they just can't keep their noses out," Hannah said.

They ran the rest of the way until they reached Hannah's

house with a couple of minutes to spare. Mrs. Fitzgerald was peeping out from behind the curtains when they returned.

"Right on schedule," Hannah grumbled.

When they caught Mrs. F's eye, she pretended she hadn't been watching at all and began vigorously cleaning the already clean windowsill.

"Club headquarters at ten tomorrow, then movies?" Chris said, and they all agreed.

AMELIA'S JOURNAL

11:35 p.m.—I can't sleep. At first, I thought it was because of the bed in my grandmother's spare room. It's all lumpy and bumpy and I don't think she's changed the mattress in about fifty years, which is kind of disgusting, but it isn't just the mattress—it's everything. I thought that coming to Newpark and staying at my gran's would be strange and it is, but EVERYTHING around here is kind of messed up. Gran was really nice when I arrived. She hugged me so tightly my bones cracked and then the three of us—me, Gran, and my dad—sat and chatted as if everything was normal, which it really isn't. Then he said good-bye and looked sort of sad and gave me a speech about being good and helping my gran because she's not getting any younger. Nobody's getting younger, Dad! If she'd hugged him, he'd see she doesn't need help—she's super-strong, like an ox or a superhero or something.

After he left, I unpacked my stuff and cried a little bit. Then I had to go down and have my lunch with Gran. She'd made stew. I <u>hate</u> stew and I don't like having my dinner in the middle of the day. Gran says she's always eaten her dinner at 1 p.m. and she's too old to change now. Then she told me to shut up with my whining.

I ate a tiny bit and when Gran wasn't looking I wrapped half of the stew in my napkin (the icky brown juices leaked through and I had to wash my hands about fifty times afterward).

Next thing, this girl Hannah comes over. I think Gran arranged for her to visit because even though I'd seen Hannah a few times I'd never spoken to her, except to say HELLO as we passed by her house. All I knew about her was that she seemed nice and didn't look like she had a clue about fashion. Turns out she IS nice (and I was right about the fashion thing, too). It was awkward at first—even though I try hard not to be, I get shy when I meet new people. My skin feels all prickly and I get really uncomfortable and I _never_ seem to say the right thing. But Gran did most of the talking so it was okay. Turns out Hannah's parents are strict, so we both have parent problems. We understand each other's pain! Then she told me she had other people to introduce me to.

Who calls themselves misfits? It's nuts, right? You might as well call yourselves losers. And even if you were a misfit, why wouldn't you cover it up and pretend to be cool? That's what I'd do, but not the Misfits Club (which I may or may not be a member of—it all got kind of muddled in the end). I don't know them well enough to know how misfitty they are, but I do know them a little bit after today's adventures.

Sam seems nice, a bit wild and he can't stop himself from saying stupid things, but he's fun. Chris, too, but he's a lot more uptight, the kind of person who always puts a coaster under a glass to stop a table from getting marked. Brian—I don't think I really like him and he DEFINITELY doesn't like me. It's like I'm crashing a party I wasn't invited to or something. I was perfectly polite, but he made a big deal of everything, said if I wanted to hang out with them I had to play this game called Gravest Danger, which sounds like the most childish thing ever, but was actually a lot of fun (not that I'd tell Brian).

The game ended up with me in this creepy cottage in the woods and it had a ghost! It was terrifying. I tried to be brave, but I was really scared. I don't like ghosts or spooky cottages or dust or spiders or dark woods, so the whole thing was like my worst nightmare.

I'm not exaggerating, but I think I barely escaped from the woods with my life.

When I got home, Gran didn't even seem to have noticed I'd been gone. She'd been busy working on the farm all afternoon and told me she thought I was sensible enough and didn't need her hovering nearby to spoil whatever fun I was having. That was a nice thing to say and if my belly hadn't been churning with sheer terror, then I would have been glad to hear it.

I called Millie, my best friend at home, and told her all about it. She said I was the bravest person she'd ever met, that if she'd been there she would have literally died, so I felt a bit better. She also said that I shouldn't go near the Misfits anymore and they sounded like trouble. I told her I had no intention of ever seeing them again.

12:05 a.m.—The thing is, if I'd been at home yesterday, my day would have been: sleep, Internet, shopping with friends, FaceTime Millie, Internet, sleep. Instead, I ran around a haunted forest and now I'm terrified. But it was exciting, too. How can I be terrified and excited at the same time?

12:11 a.m.—If I don't spend time with the Misfits, then what else am I going to do here? Help on the farm?

12:15 a.m.—I think I actually enjoyed myself yesterday.

12:33 a.m.—I just remembered something. I was taking a selfie when I heard the wail. I haven't even checked the photo gallery on my phone.

12:34 a.m.—<u>THERE'S A PICTURE OF THE GHOST ON MY PHONE!</u>

12:43 a.m.—I don't know how I got through the last few minutes without having a heart attack. I freaked out really silently. I didn't want to wake Gran. Instead of hugging me (and breaking my ribs) and telling me everything was going to be all right, she'd be the sort of person who'd take me to the woods in the middle of the night just to prove the ghost wasn't there. Even if she was right, I'd be dead with fear before I reached the cottage.

12:50 a.m.—The phone is downstairs under the cushions in the sofa. I couldn't bear to have it in the room with me in case the ghost climbed out of it and started walking toward me. I don't know why I thought I'd be safer if it was downstairs. Now I think I should have put it outside, but I can't go back downstairs. I want to stay here under the duvet where it's safe and warm. I like my lumpy bed now.

3:01 a.m.—I must have fallen asleep. How did that happen when I was so afraid? I'm awake now, though. Everything creaks in an old farmhouse. It's terrifying. Why does everything have to creak? I can't stand it! Am I being stupid?

5:16 a.m.—The rooster just crowed. I'm awake before the rooster. How crazy is that?

6:01 a.m.—Is six in the morning too early to call Hannah? I really need to talk to her. Is she one of those people who are grumpy when they're woken up? I think I should call. Do the Misfits have a WhatsApp group? I can't believe the ghost is real.

SEVEN

"Where are you going?" Brian's father asked the next morning.

Mucky must have fallen asleep on the couch again because he certainly wasn't an early riser. Even though it had almost been two years since Brian's mom had left, Mucky often preferred to spend the night on the living room couch rather than in their old bedroom.

"I'm meeting my friends," Brian said.

"Forget about your friends. I thought I told you to tidy up yesterday."

Brian *had* tidied up, but the place was a mess again. Empty cookie packets were strewn around, an overturned pizza box lay on the floor, dirty dishes were piled in the sink. Brian didn't understand how his father could make such a mess when he usually only left the couch to go to the toilet. There was no point in telling Mucky that he'd tidied up already. He'd only end up shouting at him and that would delay things. Brian wanted to catch up with the rest of the gang. He needed to know if they'd made any progress. He didn't have any credit on his phone, so he couldn't call or text them, and the phone was so ancient that he didn't have any apps to message them with—it was embarrassing.

He'd almost finished cleaning up when the doorbell rang. "Get the door," Mucky mumbled. He'd fallen asleep again.

He wiped drool from his mouth and inspected his Iron Maiden T-shirt. It was just on the right side of clean, which for Mucky meant two food stains or fewer. Iron Maiden was his favorite band. He'd seen them in concert over thirty times and still wore his hair long because he thought it made him look like the singer, Bruce Dickinson, who'd had long hair in the 1980s. Every morning Mucky combed his remaining hair across his head in the genuine belief that it prevented people from noticing he was going bald, a belief he held on to even on the days a gust of wind sent his long comb-over billowing in the air like a freshly unfurled sail.

"Get me the mouthwash," he said, jumping to his feet.

"Toothbrush and toothpaste might be better," Brian said.

"Toothbrush fell down the toilet a couple of days ago."

Brian grabbed the half-empty bottle of mouthwash from under the kitchen sink and threw it to Mucky, who took a healthy swig, swallowing some of the green liquid.

"Dad, you're not supposed to drink it. You're just supposed to swirl it around and then spit it out."

"I just figured that out," Mucky spluttered. He clawed at his tongue to get rid of some of the taste. "Oh, that's rough. It's a minty kind of hell."

The doorbell rang again. The caller was impatient. The

bell rang every three seconds, then every two seconds, and then there was no gap at all between the rings. Brian ran to answer it as Mucky spritzed his T-shirt with Febreze.

Sharon Lachey, short, skinny, and very pale, with jet-black dyed hair, was as pleased to see Brian as he was to see her, which was not very pleased at all. He'd disliked her from the moment he'd met her. She'd turned up in his life six months ago, when she'd started going out with his father. *Going out* wasn't a very accurate term. Most of the time they stayed in watching television. Sharon said she had a job, but Brian reckoned it must be part-time because she was able to come and go whenever she pleased. She never seemed short of money, though.

"You gone deaf or something?" she asked, barreling past him.

"What?" Brian said, pretending not to hear.

"I said, you gone deaf or something?" she asked again, not getting his weak attempt at a joke. "I've been ringing that doorbell for at least ten minutes. Make me a cup of tea. I'm gasping."

She plonked herself on the sofa beside Mucky, kissed him on the lips, which was enough to make Brian gag, then took the remote control from her boyfriend.

"What's that garbage?" she asked, changing the channel.

"Ah, Shar, I was watching that," he said.

She flicked through the channels until she found a program she liked. A reality show about weddings.

"Hint, hint," she said.

It took Mucky a moment to catch on.

"Ah, Shar."

"Don't *ah, Shar* me. We've being going out for six months and you're not getting any younger. I'm not going to wait around forever for my Prince Charming. And if you're going to get married again, it'd be nice if it happened while you still have some hair left on your head."

"I'm not going bald," Mucky said defiantly.

"Well, if you're not, then you'd better go to the doctor and tell him your forehead is getting bigger." She shouted over her shoulder. "Where's that cup of tea? I'm dying of thirst here."

Mucky ran his fingers through his remaining hair, as if to reassure himself it was still there.

"I don't want to bad-mouth that young fella of yours, but he's awful lazy," Sharon said.

"He gets that from his mother," Mucky said.

"About time," Sharon said as Brian arrived with two cups of tea and a packet of custard creams. "Where are the chocolate cookies? I'm not on a diet, you know."

"There's none left."

"He ate all the chocolate cookies," Sharon said to Mucky, looking shocked. "See, I told you, lazy and selfish."

Mucky had the good grace to look a little guilty. He'd been the one who'd eaten the cookies. He'd actually eaten two packets of them while watching a couple of Clint

Eastwood movies the evening before, once she'd left for work. He looked at Brian, his eyes pleading with him not to betray him to Sharon.

"Sorry about that," Brian said.

She slapped him on the belly. "Keep eating all the cookies and you'll be too fat to fit into your ring bearer outfit."

"Ring bearer? I'm twelve. I can't be a ring bearer. I'm far too old."

"If Sharon wants you to be a ring bearer, you'll be a ring bearer," Mucky said.

"But you haven't even agreed to get married yet," Brian said.

Mucky looked confused for a moment, then it seemed to dawn on him. "Oh, yeah."

"That's the kind of dress I want," Sharon said, pointing at the screen.

The woman on the screen was wearing a huge yellow dress that made her look as if she was auditioning for the part of a gigantic rubber duck. Brian didn't know much about wedding dresses, but it looked horrible to him.

"It looks expensive," Mucky said.

"Don't worry about that. I'll be coming in to some money soon."

"Really?" Mucky said, brightening up.

Sharon turned to Brian, her brow furrowing. "Can't you go to your room or something, kid? Give your old man and myself some privacy. It's rude to hang around like a bad smell."

"I'm heading out, but I'll have my phone with me so you can call if there's any more butler tasks you want me to complete," Brian said sarcastically.

"Thanks, kid," Mucky said, turning back to the TV.

Brian went around the back of the house and checked his bike. Chris had done a good job fixing it up in the ten minutes he'd had to spare before the Adamus' oh-so-important family night. Brian didn't acknowledge it, but he was a bit jealous. He was never involved in any family nights. He barely even had a family.

Since his mother had left, his father had had a few girlfriends. Most of them got tired of Mucky after a week or two; unless you enjoyed spending sixteen hours a day watching television, Mucky McDonnell wasn't exactly the greatest companion in the world. The only one who had lasted longer than Sharon—a whole six months so far—had been Marjorie. She'd been nice. Dad had started cooking when he was going out with her, and he'd even showered and shaved every single day. He'd been working at the time, but then he'd fallen out with his boss and quit his job in a temper. A couple of weeks after that, Marjorie had left. She'd kept in touch with Brian for a while, meeting up with him for hot chocolate and a chat once or twice a week, checking that his clothes were clean and that he'd done his homework. It was a pain, but a nice pain. Then she'd gotten a job in Kanturk and now they didn't see each other anymore.

The thing he didn't like to admit about Sharon was that she seemed to have a lot more in common with his dad than Marjorie had. They had the same—terrible—sense of humor, they both loved the movies of Jason Statham, and they spent hours singing along to the 1980s rock music that Mucky played at earsplitting volume. Sometimes, Brian thought there was another side to Sharon—he'd heard her answering some of the really tough questions on *Jeopardy!* once when she didn't realize he was listening—but he was probably being paranoid. He just didn't like her. He had to accept she was in his dad's life now and that Marjorie wasn't coming back. Things never stayed good for very long. They always changed.

He didn't like thinking about stuff like that, so he decided to go for a bike ride. Life was always better when he was on his bike. His phone beeped with an incoming text.

The message was from Chris:

The game is afoot.

Brian wasn't sure what that was supposed to mean. Even though they weren't due to meet up for another couple of hours, he turned his bike around and headed in the opposite direction, straight to the twins' house.

EIGHT

The Adamu home was a semidetached house in a development on the other side of the town from Brian's. Unlike Brian and Hannah, the twins had lots of brothers and sisters and their house always seemed to be overflowing with people, especially when their grandparents and cousins visited from Nigeria.

Brian flung his bike on the front walk and rang the doorbell. A couple of minutes later, the twins' father, a great big bear of a man, bleary-eyed and dressed in a T-shirt and pajama bottoms—and with amazingly bouffant bed hair—opened the door. If someone had woken Mucky too early, normally anytime before twelve, he'd have thrown a temper tantrum, but Sam and Chris's dad was a much calmer person.

"I think I should give you your own key, Brian. It'd make my life a lot easier," he said, shaking his head ruefully. "Make yourself at home. I'm going back to bed."

It was only then that Brian remembered it was the twins' father's only day off work and his one chance of sleeping in. He'd apologize later. He went into the living room and found Sam fast asleep on the couch. He often spent the night there if he fell asleep watching one of the action movies he loved so much. Brian always liked that living room. It wasn't anything like as nice as Hannah's, but it was comfortable. He felt that if he spilled or broke something while he was there that it wasn't the biggest deal in the world. The house was remarkably quiet.

He shoved at Sam's duvet-covered legs with the toe of his sneaker. His friend grunted and turned over, burying his face in a cushion. Brian tried again.

"Get lost, Chris, or I'll beat you," Sam said in a muffled voice.

"It's not Chris—it's me."

Sam sat up immediately, rubbing sleep from his eyes. "Hey, what are you doing here?"

"Text from Chris. Something about a game with a foot."

"Who knows what that guy's up to," Sam said. He climbed off the couch and went to the end of the stairs. "Chriiiis!" he roared.

"Keep it down. I'm trying to sleep," his father roared back.

"Sorry, Dad. Won't happen again," Sam shouted.

A few minutes later, Chris bounded down the stairs, his hair slicked with gel, his cheeks rosy. He was, much to Sam's irritation, a morning person.

He had a rolled-up piece of paper under his arm. "Morning," Chris said chirpily.

"Hey. What's going on?" Brian asked. "What was that text you sent me?"

"Amelia got a picture of the so-called ghost. Hannah texted me this morning."

"What?" Brian was astonished. This was a huge deal and he was only hearing about it now? "Let me see it."

"All in good time," Chris said. "Almost ready to go? Sam—hurry up and get dressed. We're meeting them in twenty minutes and then we're off to the movies. Mrs. F is going to drive us. Want to leave your bike in the back, Brian?"

"You're really not going to show me the picture? Come on, Chris, don't be a jerk."

"He can't help it—it's his default setting. I can wrestle it off him, if you like," Sam said, coming back downstairs in a clean T-shirt and grabbing a couple of jelly doughnuts and a bar of chocolate for breakfast.

"Nah, I'll wait," Brian sighed.

"Dad, we're heading out," Sam roared up the stairs. "Did you hear me? We're going to the movies."

"Of course I heard you. There are dead people who heard you. Does anyone care whether I sleep or not? Is it really too much to expect to have one morning to myself?" his father called back.

"Sorry, Dad," Sam shouted. "Forgot you were sleeping."

"I only told you two minutes ago," the twins' father wailed.

"Yeah, sorry for making all the noise," Chris bellowed.

"Me too. Didn't mean to wake you earlier," Brian roared.

They were quickly out of the door and didn't get to hear his sweary response.

Amelia and Hannah were waiting for them when they arrived. They were sitting on the wall outside Hannah's house, deep in conversation. They looked as if they had been friends forever. Amelia's eyes were red from lack of sleep and Brian thought she looked exhausted. Hannah wasn't in her usual uniform of T-shirt, jeans, and sneakers. She was a little more dressed up than she usually was, and for once her hair wasn't scraped back in a ponytail.

Chris cleared his throat, as if he was about to make a big speech.

"Before we get down to business," he began.

"Just get on with it, Chris," Brian said. "We have to talk about the ghost."

"Not here," Hannah said, looking around to check if anyone was watching her from the house. "Too much of a chance that someone's eavesdropping. We'll talk at the movie theater."

"Perfect," Chris said. "And before we discuss it we have to do things properly. This could become our first proper adventure, or mystery, or whatever, in years, and according to our constitution . . ."

He held up a document, an old school notebook. *Constitution* was too strong a word for it—it was a set of rules for the club that they'd written when they were eight years old.

"Wait," Amelia said. "Did you just say this could be your first mystery in years? I thought that all you did was investigate stuff. Isn't that why you're in the club?"

The Misfits looked sheepish.

"Weeelll," Hannah said. "To be honest, we haven't had that many mysteries recently and the ones we had . . . Let's just say they didn't work out the way we would have liked."

"They weren't that bad," Brian said defensively.

"They weren't good, buddy," Sam said.

"Remember the Case of the Missing Teapot?" Hannah asked

"What was that about?" Amelia asked.

"Pretty much what it sounds like—Mrs. Quigley had a teapot. It went missing."

"Who took it?"

"We never found out," Hannah said.

"What happened in the end?" Amelia asked.

"Mrs. Quigley bought another teapot. There's really not much of a story there."

"But that can't have been your only investigation, right? You said one of the reasons you set up the Misfits Club was to solve mysteries."

"Oh no, we had others. Remember when Sam thought aliens had invaded Newpark?" Hannah said.

"Oh yeah, that one," Chris and Brian muttered.

They both kept their heads down. Neither of them wanted to catch Amelia's eye. The alien investigation had been an all-around embarrassment. They had been younger then, but that was no excuse.

"What? There was an alien? You're joking, right?"

"Oh no, we'd never joke about alien life. Far too serious a subject," Sam said solemnly. "I had good reason to believe aliens had landed on Earth."

"You thought you saw an alien?"

"Aliens," Sam said, putting the emphasis on the plural.

"This was just after he'd seen *E.T. the Extra-Terrestrial* for the first time," Hannah said.

"Riiiiight," Amelia said slowly, drawing out the word. "And the aliens you saw looked like E.T."

Sam's eyes lit up. He was reliving the excitement of that investigation. "Not at all. That was the cool thing—they looked exactly like us. Like human beings."

Amelia paused for a moment. She looked at Sam with a quizzical expression on her narrow face. "You thought aliens were walking among us, disguised as human beings."

Sam nodded enthusiastically. "They were so lifelike."

"Sam, how did you know they weren't actually just human beings?"

"That was the tricky part."

"They *were* human beings," Hannah said.

"What about Mr. Coleman?"

"He wasn't an alien, Sam. He wasn't up to anything."

"He had a very suspicious way about him. He was always looking around him as if he thought someone was following him."

Brian had never seen Hannah look so exasperated.

"That's because *you* were following him," she said. "He had to ask your parents to stop you. Remember?"

"Even so . . ."

"Look, we're wasting time. All that stuff happened years ago, when we were little kids," Chris said. "We have a real mystery here."

"That's right," Hannah said with a smile.

"Yeah, man. The Misfits Club is back in the game," Sam said. He held up his hand for a high five, but no one took up his offer. "Aw, come on, guys, don't leave me hanging."

Brian high-fived him to keep him quiet.

"Right, and as soon as we've completed our ceremony, we can begin," Chris said.

"Come on, we don't have to do this," Hannah said.

"Oh, but we do—Brian started it by making poor Amelia go through the ritual of Gravest Danger, so we must follow things through to their logical conclusion."

Hannah sighed and turned to Amelia. "What he's saying is that this is Misfit business and we can only continue if full members of the Misfits Club are present."

"Rules are rules," said Chris.

"You're such a rebel," Sam said. "You're going to be a really fun grown-up."

Chris ignored him and continued. "Amelia passed the initiation test, but she's not yet a member of the club."

"What do I have to do now? Battle a werewolf, stake a vampire?" Amelia asked.

"Vampire staking only happens when you've been in the club for a year," Hannah said. "Stand up and raise your right hand."

Amelia, suppressing a grin, hopped off the wall and stood before Chris, who was wearing his most solemn expression—that of a grumpy judge. Sam, Brian, and Hannah had the decency to look a little humiliated.

"Sorry, Amelia, this is so embarrassing," Hannah said.

"There's nothing embarrassing about being a Misfit," Chris said.

"Most of what we do is embarrassing."

"Embarrassingly cool," Chris said.

"I blame you for this," Hannah said to Brian.

"I blame myself, too," Brian said. "Sorry, Amelia."

"Don't worry about it. I don't mind," she said. Although normally she'd have been concerned about looking foolish, now all she wanted was to get to the bottom of her ghost problem. If this is what she had to go through, then so be it.

"Okay." Chris began to read from the notebook. "Do you promise to investigate crime, fight evil, and put yourself in peril to right wrongdoings everywhere?"

"This is where you say, 'I do,'" Brian whispered.

"I do."

"Will you uphold the constitution of the Misfits Club and face down foes both natural and unnatural, human and alien, dead and undead?"

"I'm so ashamed I could vomit," Sam said.

"I will," Amelia said.

"Do you accept that to be a true Misfit, you must first be true to yourself, that you must not worry about appearing foolish, and that who you are is more important than who others want you to be?"

She hesitated a moment before answering the question.

"Yes," she said.

"Then I formally welcome you to the Misfits Club," Chris said.

"Thanks. At least there wasn't a song," Amelia joked.

"There is a song," Chris said. He began to sing. "Oooooh, Misfits, solving all your mys-ter-iiiieeees—"

He stopped when Sam smacked him on the head.

"Welcome to the coolest club on the planet, Amelia," Brian said drily.

Mrs. Fitzgerald emerged from the house and waved at them.

"Are you ready to go?" she called out.

THE CASE OF THE MISSING TEAPOT

<u>INVESTIGATORS:</u> Hannah, Sam, Chris, Brian

<u>REPORT BY:</u> Hannah

<u>CASE:</u> On Saturday, March 14, at approximately 10:45 a.m., Sam heard his neighbor, Mrs. Quigley, cry out. He reported that she shouted: "Where's my teapot gone?" Realizing that time is key in all investigations, Sam and Chris rushed over to her house at once. At first, Mrs. Quigley appeared hostile (which made Sam suspect that she might be the one behind the disappearance for insurance fraud reasons). Sam reported that she shouted: "What, in God's name, are the two of you doing in my house? I never invited you in."

Once she'd calmed down and he'd explained that they were there to help, Mrs. Quigley allowed the investigation to begin. Chris followed protocol and called in Brian and Hannah (me). We raced over to the house. Mrs. Quigley again became aggressive. "I thought you were just going to help me look for it. What's this investigating nonsense about?"

We established that the teapot in question was silver and had been bought in the 99-cent shop at some point in the previous five years. Mrs. Quigley wasn't able to give us the exact date and time of purchase. Neither was she able to provide us with a receipt to prove she'd bought it.

A thorough search of the premises revealed no sign of the teapot (although we did learn Mrs. Quigley doesn't vacuum too often). We interviewed neighbors, who were reluctant to talk, arousing suspicion, as well as the garbageman who'd collected the trash that morning. He was quite rude and remains our main suspect. After a month's investigation, we had to admit defeat. Mrs. Quigley expressed surprise when we turned up at her door to inform her of our lack of progress. "Sure, I'd forgotten all about that. I bought another teapot in the supermarket weeks ago."

MAIN SUSPECT 1: Surly garbageman (suspected by Brian, Chris, and Hannah)
MAIN SUSPECT 2: A very strong magpie, since they love shiny things (suspected by Sam)
CASE STATUS: Open

NINE

Brian was annoyed. All of this delaying before they started on their investigation was not top-notch detective work as far as he was concerned. Sherlock Holmes and Watson would never sit silently in the back of a car while they were driven to the movies by one of their friend's mothers. At least not when they had an important case to solve.

Mrs. Fitzgerald dropped them off at the door of Central Cinema, a five-screen multiplex on the edge of town.

"What time will I pick you up?" she asked through the rolled-down car window.

"We might go for a pizza after the movie," Hannah said. "I'll call you when we're ready."

"Okay. Have you got your phone? Is it charged?"

"Yes, Mom."

"And your wallet? Do you have enough money? Did you bring a pack of tissues with you?"

To Hannah's relief, a car behind her mother's Space Wagon beeped at her to drive on and she had to cut the conversation short. Hannah didn't hang around. She was through the front door and into the lobby of the theater before the others had even begun to move.

It was busier in the theater than it was in the rest of the town. Since summer vacation had started, the Central was showing films at half price every day at noon.

The smell of freshly popped popcorn hung deliciously in the air.

"Are we actually going to watch a movie?" Amelia asked.

"We have to. Just in case my mother checks me for ticket stubs afterward and asks what the movie was about. I'll get the tickets," Hannah said.

Brian knew what she was doing. Anytime he didn't have enough money, which was quite often these days, Hannah seemed to sense it. She'd pay for things so he didn't have to embarrass himself by searching his pockets for money he knew wasn't there. She always looked out for him.

He was distracted from his thoughts by a familiar squeaky voice.

"Hey, guys."

Horace McCarthy was a small, nervous boy who was in Brian's class in school. He was always deathly pale and his resting facial expression was *seriously worried.*

"Hey, Horace," Sam said cheerfully as Hannah returned with the tickets.

"What are you guys going to see?" Horace asked.

"*Mouse Number 72,*" Hannah said.

"I thought we were going to see *The Mystery of Banshee Towers*," Chris said.

"Yeah, *Mouse Number 72*'s a kids' movie," Sam moaned. "If anyone sees me going into that, my reputation will be ruined. People think I'm cool, y'know."

"Oh, Sam, they really don't," Chris said, giving his brother a sympathetic pat on the shoulder.

"What are you going to see, Horace?" Brian asked.

"*Zombie Bloodfest 2: The Ripping*," Horace squeaked. "My brother's an usher here, so he lets me in. He used to work with my dad in the gift shop, but he got fired for being useless."

"Isn't that movie a little gory for you?" Hannah asked.

"It is if *Zombie Bloodfest 1* is anything to go by. I was so terrified the night I saw it I couldn't even cross the hall to the bathroom even though I really needed to pee."

Hannah introduced him to Amelia. "She's the newest member of our club."

Horace looked crestfallen, but he tried to cover it up.

"I didn't realize the Misfits Club was taking on new members," he said, his eyes watering a little. "Good for you, Amelia. You'll have fun. I always thought—"

"Looks like you're not the only zombie fan today," Brian said, interrupting.

Declan Grabbe, aka Smasher, was heading into theater number two, the theater that was showing Horace's zombie film. If Horace hadn't been deathly pale already, his face would have drained of color at that moment.

Smasher was a year older than Brian and had been in elementary school with him until the year before. He'd hit a growth spurt when he'd turned thirteen and could now easily pass for a very large adult or a small house.

"He's huge," Amelia gasped.

"And that's when he's far away. Up close he's absolutely enormous," Brian said.

Smasher's distinguishing characteristic was that he believed violence was the answer to every problem. He was followed into the screening by Kelly and Conway. Their distinguishing characteristics were that they were the only two people in school who didn't find Smasher's company repulsive.

"Don't worry, I'm sure your brother will keep an eye out for you," Chris said.

"Not a chance. My brother's even wimpier than I am. I'd better go in and make sure I'm sitting as far away from Smasher as possible. The last thing I need is to get on his bad side," Horace said. "Catch you later."

"Suddenly, *Mouse Number 72* doesn't seem that bad a choice," Sam said.

"Why did you choose that movie anyway?" Amelia asked.

"Because we can talk in there and not annoy anyone," Hannah said.

A couple of minutes later, the other Misfits understood what she meant. The theater was filled with screaming babies, whimpering toddlers, and wild five-year-olds energized by excessive intakes of sugar. Most of the parents would have preferred to be anywhere else in the world than where they were at that very moment. They were weary and red-eyed and Brian thought some of them looked as if they were on the verge of screaming themselves.

"Okay, good choice," Chris said. "We can talk as much as we want here and nobody'll notice."

They settled into some seats near the back.

"Anyone got any popcorn?" Sam asked.

"I've got a bag of gummi snakes," Amelia said. She opened the bag and held it out. "Anyone want one?"

"I *love* gummi snakes," Brian said, taking a handful. *Maybe this Amelia girl isn't so bad after all*, he thought. Anyone who loved gummi snakes was all right in his book.

"Focus, guys," Hannah said as the lights went down and the trailers began to play on the screen. The booming noise from the speakers wasn't enough to drown out all the screaming and crying.

Chris unrolled the poster he'd been guarding as if it was the most important thing ever. It was a grainy, blown-up version of the photograph Amelia had taken in the cottage in the woods. Sam took out his phone and switched on the flashlight function to make sure everyone could see the poster. As far as Amelia was concerned, the light only made things worse.

"You can see right up my nostrils," she gasped.

It was the first thing she'd noticed.

"At least you didn't have any boogers. They'd have been magnified, too. It wouldn't have been a pretty sight," Brian said.

"Are you nuts? Giant boogers would have been awesome," Sam said.

"Forget about Amelia's nose—"

"I don't have boog—" Amelia began.

"—and focus on the rest of the picture," Hannah said.

The rest of the picture was part of the fireplace, the window to the left, and beyond that the small clearing that had once been the back garden. At the edge of the clearing lay the fuzzy figure that was perplexing them. He was hollow-cheeked and wore a hoodie that obscured his face and a pair of dark-colored gloves on his hands.

"Man, that is one ugly old ghost," Sam said.

"It's not a ghost," Hannah said. "Look at his clothes. They're modern."

"Maybe he's just a fashionable kind of ghost," Sam said.

"No," Hannah said. "It's a man. I'm Irish and I'm Vietnamese and both sides love wandering spirits and ghouls, but I'm a detective, too, so I have to be sensible and look at the facts. No matter how much I'd love it to be a ghost, I still think it's a man."

Sam sighed. "I was really hoping it'd be a ghost, too. That would have been awesome. I really wanted us to have one cool investigation before we left."

Brian's heart sank. He hated it when either of the twins mentioned they were leaving. It was horrible.

"What was in the woods yesterday may not have been a ghost, but I don't think that man was up to any good. Why would he be lurking around the woods like that?" Chris asked.

"*We* were lurking around the woods," Sam said reasonably.

"But he's wearing a hoodie and gloves and it wasn't even cold yesterday," Hannah pointed out.

"And he wailed and threw something at the wall when he saw my phone flash," Amelia said.

"You mentioned that yesterday. You're certain he wailed?"

"There was definite wailage. You don't wail when you think you've been photographed, unless you're up to no good," Amelia said.

"We shouldn't be sitting here half-watching a movie for toddlers—we should be out there finding out what he was up to," Brian said.

"He's right," Hannah said. "Let's go."

They didn't waste any more time hanging around the theater. They bustled their way through the crowds of children playing in the aisle and made their way to the lobby.

As they were about to leave, Brian spotted Horace McCarthy hiding behind a large cardboard cutout of a family of aliens. Horace was looking even paler than he had earlier, if that was possible.

"Everything okay, Horace?" Brian asked.

"Not really. Smasher's after me. You guys were right. *Zombie Bloodfest 2* was too gory for me. I felt nauseous, so I decided to leave. I didn't make it to the bathroom in time. I got sick."

"Why would that matter to Smasher?"

"I got sick on his shoes. My brother tried to help, but Smasher stuffed him in a trash can. He's stuck in there now."

"Act casual," Chris whispered.

Smasher was on the far side of the lobby, his face as twisted as an outraged demon's. He looked as if he was ready to mangle anything or anyone who got in his way.

"Don't worry, Horace," Brian said. "We're going to get you out of here."

"I appreciate the words of comfort, but I *am* worried, Brian. Look at him. He's like a monster disguised as a teenager. I'm mincemeat."

Brian's glare quieted him. He turned to his fellow Misfits.

"All right, here's the plan: You four are going to stick close together and Horace is going to hide behind you. Provide cover for him until we get outside. If Smasher heads our way, I'll create a distraction."

"How?" Amelia asked.

Smasher *was* heading in their direction, growing larger and more menacing with every step he took.

"Probably by getting severely injured," Brian said. "Okay, move it."

Smasher was halfway across the lobby when Brian stepped forward to meet him as the other four, standing closely together, began to shuffle sideways, like a group of crabs, from the cardboard cutout to the theater's front door. Horace had ducked down low behind them, waddling along on his haunches, terrified that his pounding heartbeat would attract the attention of his enemy.

"Hey, Declan," Brian said chirpily. "How's it going?"

It took a moment for Smasher to realize someone was talking to him. He looked down at Brian.

"Remember me?" Brian said. "No? I was a year behind you in school. You were in Ms. Knightl—"

"You seen a small vomity guy?" Smasher said, his voice deep and resonant.

"Nope, can't say I have," Brian replied.

"Then get out of my way."

"He's here," came an excited shout.

Kelly and Conway, Smasher's friends, had spotted Horace lurking behind the Misfits. They'd almost made it as far as the door, but almost wasn't enough.

Smasher was about to lurch forward when he felt a grip

on his arm. Brian was doing his best to hold him back. It wasn't a very effective tactic.

"You've just made a huge mistake," Smasher said.

"Think I've realized that now," Brian said, but he didn't release his grip on the large teenager.

At the same time, Kelly and Conway were trying to push their way through the Misfits to get to Horace. The Misfits were putting up a fight, but the others were stronger. It was only a matter of time before they broke through.

"Tell my parents I loved them and that I want to be buried at sea," Horace squeaked.

Smasher easily pried Brian's fingers from his arm, then grabbed him by the collar of his T-shirt, lifting him up so that Brian's legs dangled in the air. Even in the midst of his fear, he could smell the foul stench from Smasher's shoes.

Oh, Horace, you idiot, Brian thought.

"Let him go," Hannah shouted at Smasher. She'd broken away from the group, and her rebellion was enough to surprise Kelly and Conway into stopping for a moment.

A slow, nasty smirk spread across Smasher's flat features. "Let him go, or what?"

"Or you'll have me to deal with," Hannah said, striking a karate pose.

"Oooh, I'm scared. Get lost, girly," Smasher said dismissively.

"I've been training since the age of three," Hannah said.

"I'm a fourth Dan black belt and I know two types of secret death grips that my grandfather passed on to me. If you think I'm lying, why don't you try me? Or are you worried about being beaten up by a girl?"

"You can't win, Smasher," Brian said. "Even if you don't lose the fight, you'll be known around town as the huge guy that beat up a girl. Walk away."

Smasher Grabbe considered it for a moment. The short guy was right—that wouldn't do his reputation any good at all. He released his grip on Brian, who dropped to the ground with a graceless thump.

"You two," he grunted at Kelly and Conway. "Leave them alone."

"But, Smasher—" Kelly began.

"I said, leave them alone." He turned to Horace. "I'll see you again. Very soon."

Horace began to tremble.

"I'll see you again, too," Smasher said to Brian. "You won't know where and you won't know when—"

"Probably around town since we both live here," Brian said.

A vein began to throb in Smasher's temple.

"Why are you antagonizing him?" Chris whispered.

"I don't know. It's a kind of sickness," Brian said.

"Next time your Chinese friend won't be around to save you," Smasher said.

"I'm Irish, you jerk," Hannah said.

Amelia began to usher her friends toward the door. "Right, now's the time to go, while we're still alive and have all of our limbs."

She made sure that Horace left before them and he ran home faster than he'd ever, or would ever, run in his life.

"Remember when you said nothing happened around here?" Chris said.

"Yeah, with all the ghosts and thugs and stuff, I may have to revise that opinion," Sam said.

"Do you really know karate?" Amelia asked.

"Never had one lesson," Hannah replied.

"I don't know about you," Sam said, "but I think we all need to go and sit somewhere comfortable and eat a bunch of burgers."

"Are you nuts?" Brian said. "I'm not hanging around any longer. We're going back to the woods and we're going now."

TEN

Chris found the woods a lot creepier than he had the day before. He'd been intrigued by the possibility of a mystery and he loved investigating, but the parts he liked most were research, deduction, and the use of logic. What he didn't like was wandering around the woods with a potentially dangerous man on the loose, a man who clearly didn't want them around. He couldn't understand why the others were all so excited about checking it out. Hadn't they ever watched a movie before? Things always ended badly for people who went investigating by themselves in dark woods.

"What did you tell your mother?" Amelia asked.

"I told her Sam and Chris's parents were dropping us at the end of the road and then I was going over to your grandmother's house," Hannah replied.

"What if she looks for you there?"

"Florence is always out in the fields doing something. The chances of catching her at home are slim. And, to be honest, Mom's not likely to call over. She's scared of your gran."

"She can be a little scary."

"I think she's cool," Hannah said.

It wasn't as dark in the forest as it had been the previous afternoon, but they'd still brought along a huge flashlight, which Sam had liberated from a kitchen cupboard. They needed the light to help them pick their way through the roots and brambles, which they'd all tripped over running away in terror the day before. They'd been in a hurry to get going, so despite Chris's pleadings there hadn't been enough time to work out any kind of detailed plan.

"There's no need," Brian had said. "We go into the cottage, have a look around. See if there's anything odd that we didn't see before. Look for clues. That's it."

They reached the cottage within a few minutes and Chris gasped.

"What's wrong now?" Sam sighed.

"Look." He was standing at the front door, examining the handle. The others crowded around him.

"What are we supposed to be looking at?" Sam asked.

Hannah answered the question for him. "There's a padlock on the door. There wasn't a lock there yesterday."

The padlock had a thick brass body and a silver shackle. Brian knew that no one would go to the trouble of putting one on the door unless they had something to hide.

"We could try to pick the lock. Well, I can't, but you could, Chris. You watched all those YouTube videos, right, that time we were investigating the Mystery of the Houdini Goat?" Brian said.

Amelia opened her mouth to speak, but Hannah cut her off.

"Don't ask," she said.

"You know how to do it, don't you?" Brian continued.

Chris did remember. When he studied something, he really put his heart and soul into it and when it came to things like watching *How To* videos he had a perfect memory. That wasn't the problem. The problem was that it didn't feel like the right thing to do. They suspected the man was up to no good, but that didn't give them the right to just break into the cottage, did it?

"Give me a second. I need to think about this," Chris said.

We should really tell someone, he thought. But would anyone take them seriously? They could always ask their cousin, Debra. She was an officer of the law. She'd listen to them. It was definitely a matter for the authorities. Yet, on the other hand, if he didn't pick the lock, then he'd be letting his friends down. It'd been ages since their previous investigation, and this was likely to be their very last one before the club disbanded and his family moved to Galway. No, he still couldn't do it, he decided. The Misfits Club upheld the law; it didn't break the l—

"I'm in."

When Chris turned around, the lock was on the ground, a chunk of the door was missing, and Sam was standing there, an odd expression on his face and a rock in his hand. He'd bashed his way in.

"I only gave it a tap," Sam said. "We must have softened it up yesterday when Amelia got stuck in there."

"Oh, we're going to get in so much trouble," Chris said with a forlorn shake of his head.

"I had to do it," Sam said. "This isn't like homework or eating healthily—this is important."

"Don't worry about it now," Hannah said.

"Don't worry about it? How can you be so calm? We're literally at the halfway point of breaking and entering," Chris said. He took a deep breath. "Okay, guys, the breaking has been done. Nothing we can do about that now. These things happen. As long as we don't follow the breaking with some entering, then we can sort—"

Sam was leading the way. He pushed the door open.

"Do not go in there. As your older brother, I forbid you to go into that cottage."

Sam stepped inside and was quickly followed by Brian, Hannah, and Amelia.

"What's wrong with all of you? Don't you understand what *forbidding* means? We're supposed to be detectives, not criminals."

There was no reply. They were ignoring him. He let out an involuntary scream when a rabbit surprised him by gently bunny-hopping into the clearing. Chris had the decency to look embarrassed about it. He really was on edge.

"Nobody heard that squeal? No? Good, good. I can still

pretend I have some self-respect," he muttered. "Hello there, little guy."

The rabbit stared back at him.

"This place is creepier than I remember," Hannah said, brushing aside a thick curtain of cobwebs from her face as she reached the living room with the fireplace. "You did well to stay in here for almost five minutes, Amelia."

"It wasn't that bad," Amelia said, hoping the others didn't notice the shakiness in her voice.

"No, I agree with Hannah. You did well," Brian said.

As Hannah and Amelia began their examination of the living room, Brian and Sam made their way into what had once been the kitchen.

"Can we finish up? I have things to do," Chris shouted from outside.

"You can tidy your room and iron your jeans later," Sam said. He turned to the others. "I know he's my brother and I'm legally obliged to love him, but sometimes he really gets on my nerves."

Twenty minutes later, after a thorough examination, the four inside the cottage still hadn't found anything.

"We've checked everywhere and we haven't come across one suspicious item," Hannah said. "How's that for bad luck?"

"Any chips left?" Brian asked.

"What about the attic?" Chris shouted. "Did you check there?"

He'd grown bored and was sitting on the ground outside the cottage, aiming the flashlight in the direction of anything that moved or appeared to move. He still didn't like the idea of them breaking and entering, but he hated the idea of them finding absolutely nothing even more.

"Is there an attic?"

"It's got a peaked roof and low ceilings, right? That means there's space overhead. It may not be used, but it could be an attic."

"I'm on it," Hannah said.

They searched everywhere they thought an attic door might be located and were about to give up when Amelia spotted it in the gloom. A tiny circle, no more than a groove in the kitchen ceiling. A little brass ring that had been painted the same color white as the kitchen had once been.

"There," she cried. She lit it up with the beam from her phone flashlight.

Sam pulled across a creaking rickety chair, stood on it, and reached up toward the ring.

"If it hasn't been used in years, it'll be stuck," Hannah said.

But as soon as he slipped his fingers around it and pulled, it gave way. The attic door swung down, barely missing Sam's nose, and leaving a dark space in the ceiling above them.

Brian knew that if it opened that easily, it had been used recently. Someone else had been up there. His heart gave a jolt. What if that person was still there, hiding? Before Brian had a chance to warn him to look out, Sam was hauling himself up.

Brian tried to follow him, but, because he was shorter than Sam, his fingers wouldn't reach the edge of the attic entrance no matter how far he stretched or how many toes he tippy-toed on.

Sam coughed and spluttered as he clambered into the dusty attic, careful to balance on the beams and not put any body weight on the spaces in between. If he did, he'd end up crashing through the ceiling in a cloud of plaster, dust, and broken limbs.

"Anyone else coming up?" he shouted down.

"Nah, I think you've got it covered," Brian said, getting off the chair. "I might just check the rest of the cottage again in case we missed anything."

"Good idea. Mind if I follow Sam up there?" Hannah asked.

"Why would I mind?" Brian replied, a little testily.

Sam and Hannah crawled across the narrow attic on their hands and knees. The thin light from Hannah's phone barely disturbed the darkness. Much to their disappointment, the attic appeared to be empty.

Sam was about to roar at Chris to bring in the large

flashlight when Hannah squealed. She'd suddenly thought of something she hadn't wanted to think about.

"What if there are rats up here?" she said. "I'm not a big fan of rats."

"More likely to be mice," Sam said.

"Mice, I can handle. Mice are cute as buttons. It's rats I can't stand," she said with a shudder.

"Why are girls always so scared of rats? It makes no sense," Sam said.

"You're not scared of anything, I suppose?" Hannah said.

"Fear is for wimps," Sam said.

"So, you're not worried about the three large spiders on your shoulders then," Hannah said.

"Yeaarrrggh, get 'em off, get 'em off," Sam cried, jumping to his feet.

In his blind panic, he'd forgotten where he was and that the roof was much closer to his head than it would be under normal circumstances. His forehead cracked on a thick wooden beam, which was enough to dislodge the spiders from his T-shirt. They landed softly on the floor and scurried into the dark recesses of the attic, barely avoiding being squashed by Sam's body as it collapsed like a felled tree.

"*Aaargh*," Sam said as he landed awkwardly.

Hannah crawled to his side. "Are you okay?" she asked.

"I said 'aaargh.' It's kind of well-known as a word that indicates pain," Sam said.

Amelia couldn't see what was going on, but guessed from the anguished cries that all was not well.

"Is someone hurt?" she shouted up through the attic hatch.

"I can't really tell because of all the agony," Sam replied.

"We're fine," Hannah shouted back.

"Speak for yourself," Sam said with a grimace.

He was about to launch into an explanation of the seven different kinds of pain he was in when he distracted himself. From his prone position, he was viewing the roof from a different angle and he'd noticed something he hadn't seen before.

"Hey, shine the light up there."

Hannah moved the light beam around until she saw what he was pointing to.

"Holy moly, this just got interesting," she cried out.

"What's going on?" Brian shouted.

It was a good minute before he received a reply.

"We've got ourselves a proper mystery," Hannah said.

ELEVEN

Sam, swiftly forgetting all about the pain he'd been in, dropped from the attic back into the kitchen, quickly followed by Hannah. They rushed outside with Brian and Amelia to where Chris was anxiously pacing up and down. All at once, everyone was talking over each other, asking questions, making faces, and waving arms, without a single person able to understand a word any of the others were saying.

"Okay, okay, one at a time, or we're not going to get anywhere," Hannah shouted.

She had to repeat herself a number of times before she got them to calm down a little.

"What did you find?" Chris asked, his eyes wide with excitement.

"There's a secret door in the attic and there's stuff up there," Hannah said.

"A secret door? Are you serious? That's awesome."

"What kind of stuff? Is it money? Are we rich?" Brian asked.

"I didn't see any money. There's a painting of a ship, some bits of old jewelry, and—"

"What kind of jewelry?" Amelia asked.

"There's a necklace and some earrings—"

"And there's, like, a lamp that looks really old, too."

"Oh, so it's just the kind of junk people keep in an attic," Brian said.

"No, it didn't look like junk to me. Definitely not," Hannah said.

"No way, José, this was good stuff. It looked like a real painting, you know, one painted by a serious painter," Sam said.

"When did you become an art expert?" Chris said.

"Not now, Chris. This is serious. I think it's been stolen. There's no other reason for it to be hidden there, right?" Hannah said.

"I have to have a look," Brian said.

Hannah grabbed him before he was through the door. "Wait, we need to decide what we're going to do. The guy who put the lock on the door could be back at any minute, right? We can't spend hours examining the stuff when we should be doing something else."

"Like what?" Brian asked. He really wanted to see what they'd found, even if he had to shame himself by asking Sam for a boost up into the attic.

This was bigger than any of them had expected.

"Did you touch anything?" Chris asked.

"No, of course not," Sam lied. "How stupid do you think we are?"

He exchanged a look with Hannah. He knew that the last thing any of them needed right now was his brother freaking out.

"Okay, then there's only one thing to do," Chris said.

"Don't say 'tell our parents,'" Brian said.

"That's exactly what I'm going to say. It's the only answer, guys. If what's up there actually is stolen, then that man Amelia photographed could be a dangerous criminal. We can't just take this on by ourselves."

"Of course we can," Sam said. "We're a club that tries to get to the bottom of mysterious stuff and you want to run to Mom the first time we have something to investigate since I saw the aliens."

"Sam's right. Not about the aliens, but the rest of it. We can deal with this. It's the opportunity we've been waiting for," Hannah said. "It's like fate or something. We'd be idiots not to look into it."

"We'd also be idiots if we got captured or beaten up or worse," Chris said.

"What's wrong with you?" Sam said. He threw his hands in the air in exasperation. "Why do you have to be safe and boring like some wrinkly thirty-year-old?"

"Someone needs to engage their brain and act sensibly."

"Yeah, but why does it always have to be you?" Sam said.

"There's no way my parents are finding out about this," Hannah said.

"Fine, but if we're not telling parents then I think we should compromise and tell Debra," Chris said.

"Compromise? Let's just ignore him," Sam said to Hannah. "Come on, we'll—"

"We're a club, Sam. We have to do it together or not at all."

"Yeah, well, let's form a new club," Sam said. Hannah gave him a look and Sam knew there was no point fighting.

"Who's Debra?" Amelia asked.

"Debra's sort of related to us. She's married to my dad's first cousin and she's a cop in town. We could talk to her. She's cool," Chris said.

"Fine. I can't stop you from telling Debra, but I'm not going with you. I'm staying here," Brian said.

"Me too," Hannah said.

"Well, if you two are staying then so am I," Sam said.

"You can't. You'll need to act as a guide for Amelia and Chris. Amelia doesn't know her way out of the woods and Chris could get lost in an empty room—"

"Hey," Chris protested.

"I'm not being mean. You have a terrible sense of direction," Brian said.

"I know, but still."

"Fine, I'll go with them," Sam said, "but I've got a bad feeling about this."

"What kind of bad feeling?" Hannah asked.

"A *bad* one."

"Thanks for clearing it up."

Sam, Chris, and Amelia set off for the police station, a walk of almost two miles, while Hannah and Brian stayed behind at the cottage. After numerous failed attempts at boosting Brian into the attic, they shut the door, then spent time walking around the outside of the cottage, looking for anything that might be considered a clue. They chatted excitedly, neither of them fully able to believe that the Misfits Club had finally found itself a good old-fashioned mystery.

Their excitement faded a few minutes later when they heard the voices.

Men's voices.

THE NEWPARK ECHO

Thursday, March 14

CATS & ROBBERS: DARING RESCUE ATTEMPT LEADS TO TREE-MENDOUS EMBARRASSMENT

There was laughter in court today when new police recruit Debra O'Loughlin (27) gave evidence in the trial of two Cork men. Officer O'Loughlin had been on foot patrol in the Lavally Upper area when she noticed two middle-aged men standing beside a large white van parked on the sidewalk outside a bungalow belonging to Mr. Max Leahy. She approached the men, who told her they'd been helping Mr. Leahy move when they'd heard a cat meowing. It appeared that a ginger cat, known to locals as Lumpy, had become trapped in a nearby tree. The men said he had been stuck there for at least an hour, but since neither of them had a head for heights they'd been unable to help the poor creature.

Luckily for the adventurous Lumpy, the young officer wasn't about to leave him in the lurch. O'Loughlin outlined in court how she'd attempted to rescue the cat: "The two men, whom I now know to be Mr. Gillespie and Mr. Sweeney, took a ladder from Mr. Leahy's backyard and secured it against the tree. I climbed up as far as the ladder would take me and then began to haul myself up the tree until I reached Lumpy.

"I took the cat in my arms and, while sitting on a branch, began to pet his head to soothe him," O'Loughlin read from her evidence notebook. "At this point, I heard muttering from below, followed by a scraping sound." After questioning from the prosecuting lawyer, Mr. Randal O'Connor, it was established that the scraping sound was caused by Gillespie and Sweeney removing the ladder and leaving O'Loughlin stranded in the tree.

"I shouted at them to put the ladder back, but they responded with rude gestures. I then came to the conclusion that they were not actually friends of Mr. Leahy, as they had claimed."

"How did you arrive at that conclusion?" Mr. O'Connor asked.

"By observing them stealing many items from his house. I was unable to call for help as Lumpy was still shaking in my arms and I couldn't reach my radio. I was afraid that if I tried I would overbalance and that the two of us would fall out of the tree. Shortly afterward, Mr. Leahy returned home and confirmed my suspicions by shouting: 'I've been robbed. They've taken everything. Absolutely everything.' He was not amused when he spotted me sitting in a tree stroking a nervous cat's head."

At this point, laughter broke out in court and Judge Edan Keenan had to call for silence a number of times before things finally calmed down, following the ejection of two members of the public who were unable to stop snickering.

Officer O'Loughlin and Lumpy were rescued from the tree shortly after Mr. Leahy's return. Gillespie and Sweeney were found guilty and received sentences.

TWELVE

The two officers couldn't stop laughing. The older one's belly jiggled while tears streamed down the younger one's face.

"You . . . Let me get this right . . . You want us to investigate a house in the woods, where you think a ghost has hidden some treasure?"

The police station was small, and appeared even smaller with three members of the Misfits Club squashed into the narrow public area on the other side of the counter from the two officers. The older one was Sergeant Calvin Macklow and Sam recognized the younger one—he was Sam's PE teacher's boyfriend—his name was Tim or Jim or something like that.

"Would you look at them. They think they're the Hardy Boys and Nancy Drew," Sergeant Macklow said. "Thanks for livening up what has been a very dull day."

"Look, if we could just talk to Debra . . . I mean, Officer O'Loughlin, then we could get this all cleared up quite quickly," Chris said.

"Is he here?" Tim (or was it Jim?) asked.

"Is who here?"

The younger man wafted his hands around in a floaty manner. "The ghost. Is he here now, in the station, but I just can't see him? Do you have to be psychic to see him?"

"Remember I said that my pen had gone missing this morning," the sergeant said. "Maybe the ghost took it."

It was fair to say it wasn't going well. They'd asked for Debra twice already, but the officers weren't in any hurry to call her. Amelia knew their mistake had been to let Sam speak first. As soon as they'd arrived at the station, Chris and Amelia had clammed up in the unfamiliar environment, but Sam had marched up to the counter and begun talking. It had been proceeding in a relatively normal manner until he mentioned the word *ghost*. As soon as that word had popped out of his mouth, the two officers, who had previously seemed desperately bored, had shown a sudden interest in what he had to say. Tim/Jim had made cups of tea and the two officers of the law had pulled up seats and listened with an increasing amount of mirth as Sam had told the story. When they'd shown them the picture that Amelia had taken on her phone, they'd started to refer to the man in the photo as Casper the Friendly Ghost.

Amelia had kept quiet, but the mocking laughter annoyed her so much she'd begun clenching and unclenching her fists without even being aware of it.

"He didn't say a ghost had stolen anything," Chris said.

"He said that we suspected it was a ghost, but then we realized it wasn't. And then we found the treasure in the attic."

"So you're telling me that if I go to this cottage in the woods, and I climb into the attic, I'll see a pile of treasure?"

"Yes," Sam exclaimed. "That's exactly what we're saying."

"Is it pirate treasure? Did Casper join up with Long John Silver and Captain Jack Sparrow?"

The sergeant took a hearty slurp of milky tea, some of the liquid dribbling down his chin and onto the front of his uniform. The door to the back office opened.

"Chris? Sam? What are you doing here? Is everything okay?" Debra O'Loughlin asked. She was tall and rosy-cheeked, and her eyes were filled with a steely determination.

Once she'd been reassured that her cousins-in-law were in good health, the sergeant quickly filled her in on what had happened so far.

"So what do you think, Officer O'Loughlin?" he asked, turning to Debra. "This case sounds like a priority to me. I think we should investigate it immediately. And by *we*, I mean *you*."

"I don't think there's any need to go that far, Sergeant," Debra said.

"Oh, I disagree. This could be the important next step in your career. You've a reputation to uphold. You've already saved a cat . . . What was his name . . . ? Bumpy, was it?"

"Lumpy, I believe," the younger officer said.

"That's it. One moment you're saving good old Lumpy, the next you could be thwarting a team of thieving ghosts," he chuckled. "That's enough to put you in . . . high spirits."

"What's wrong with you? We already told you it wasn't a ghost," Sam said.

The sergeant's eyes narrowed. "Don't talk to me like that, son."

Chris nudged his brother sharply.

"Sorry," Sam muttered. He didn't sound sorry at all.

"Did any of you take a photo of this treasure?" Debra O'Loughlin asked.

"I wasn't in the attic," Amelia said.

"Why didn't you take one, Sam?" Chris said.

"How could I take one? I was practically unconscious after I banged my head. I'm lucky to be alive," Sam replied.

Debra rolled her eyes. This was promising to be a very long day.

"What are you waiting for, Officer O'Loughlin? Off you go with the boys and girl. They'll love a spin in the patrol car."

"You're not serious, are you?" Debra said.

"Very serious. You know me. I never joke about anything."

"But, I have to—"

"That can wait. Like I said, priority case. Off you go now. That's a direct order. You can give us a full report when you return. We'll hold the fort here. And don't worry—we'll keep the radio on, so if you encounter anything spooky or otherworldly you can let us know immediately."

"And, if you do meet the ghost, check that he has a haunting license. Like a hunting license? Geddit?"

The sergeant opened his mouth so widely that Amelia thought he was going to swallow his entire mug of tea. He inhaled deeply before exploding in spluttering laughter, sending showers of spittle and cold tea across the station.

"Eeeurgh, I think some of it landed on me," Amelia said as they walked toward the patrol car. She took a brand-new tissue from a pack she always carried with her and began to wipe her hair.

They climbed into the car. It was the first time any of them had ever been in a patrol car.

"This is cool," Sam said. "Can I sit in the front seat?"

Debra O'Loughlin sighed. "I only have two rules for traveling in my car. Rule number one is no one speaks. Not a single word. Obey rule number one and we'll all get along just fine."

"What's the second rule?"

"You've just violated rule number one."

"What was the first rule again?" Sam asked.

Debra shook her head sadly. When she was young, she had dreamed of becoming a detective after watching lots and lots of crime shows. She'd been expecting a few dull jobs early on in her career. What she hadn't expected was that she'd be doing things like this. Why hadn't she applied to work in Dublin or London or Los Angeles? Almost nothing ever happened in Newpark. And the one time it had she'd become the laughingstock of the town. How was that for bad luck? Now here she was driving some kids around, kids that were talking about ghosts and treasure. That it was the most exciting job she'd had in weeks only made her more depressed.

As soon as Hannah and Brian had heard the men's voices, they did the first thing that came into their heads—they ran into the cottage and hid behind the shabby old living-room sofa. On reflection, it may not have been their best-ever plan. Unless they decided to crash through the windows like stunt doubles in a thriller movie, their only exit was the door they'd just come through. They were trapped.

"We shouldn't have come in here," Hannah whispered.

"I know, but—" Brian began.

He didn't get to finish the sentence. The door of the cottage creaked open.

"Someone's been here," a man's voice said.

"Are you sure?" the second man said. His voice was deeper.

"They broke the lock."

"Might just have been some kids messing around."

"Check if anything's missing."

"Why do I have to check?"

"Because I told you to."

Hannah and Brian kept low behind the couch. It was about five feet from the back wall of the living room, not visible at first glance from the doorway, but if anyone ventured halfway across the room? Both of them held their breath and tried not to move. They couldn't see either of the men, but they sounded rough, and, to Brian at least, their voices sounded a little bit familiar, even if he couldn't quite place them.

Brian had to bite his tongue to stop himself from shouting when he saw what Hannah was up to. She was crawling on her belly toward the end of the couch, trying to peer out and catch a glimpse of the men.

Moving as silently as he could across the cold and dirty floor, he reached out and grabbed her by the ankle to stop her progress. She turned back when she felt his grip, an annoyed look on her face. He shook his head, telling her no, that it was safer to stay where they were. She mimed at him to let go of her leg.

Before they could continue their silent argument, they heard the men stomp down the short hallway toward the kitchen, making quite a racket. When the two men spoke again, their voices were a little fainter, but still clear.

"Watch that ladder. You're wrecking the place."

"Who cares? It's not like anyone lives here."

They heard the attic door swing open. Brian was just glad they'd decided to shut it earlier, otherwise the men would have known someone had been up there. That was a lucky break.

The two Misfits looked at each other. A silent misunderstanding passed between them.

"We can't let them take the stuff. If they disappear with it, we might never find them again," Hannah whispered.

"We have to get out of here first," Brian whispered back. "We can't do anything if we're trapped or kidnapped."

"I don't have time to argue with you," Hannah whispered. "So we'll go with my plan."

"How is that going to work?"

Hannah shrugged. She didn't have the answer just yet. She wondered how long it would take the others to return with reinforcements. Brian seemed to have read her mind correctly this time.

"The earliest they'll be back here is about twenty minutes from now," he whispered.

As far as Hannah was concerned, that was too long. She wasn't going to wait. She took her mobile phone from her pocket. Brian began waving at her, warning her not to use it. She made the phone call signal, shook her head no, then pretended to tap the keys. He understood what she was saying—she wasn't going to call anyone, she was going to text. Get the others to call someone in authority if they had to, to let them know that the criminals—if that's what they were—were here and were about to take all the evidence with them.

Brian was nervous. He knew by the tense expression on Hannah's face that she was nervous as well, but it wasn't stopping her.

She was about to begin texting when her phone rang.

THIRTEEN

Amelia had enjoyed the looks they'd gotten from passers-by as they'd driven down Newpark's long main street. Some people had seemed shocked to see three children in the back of a patrol car.

The traffic was heavy at the end of town, but soon they were out in the countryside, the housing developments giving way to trees and fields where, every so often, they'd see a tractor pulling a two-wheeled machine that spat out round hay bales.

"Any chance you could put the siren on, Deb?" Sam asked.

"What did I tell you about talking?"

"That you love the sound of my voice?"

"Sam."

"Shutting up now."

The patrol car took a left turn. Sam and Chris exchanged a look, Chris raising a quizzical eyebrow. This wasn't the route they'd have chosen.

"I know what I'm doing," Debra said. "This is a shortcut.

It'll only be a fifteen-minute walk from where I'll park. We'll be there soon enough."

Hannah managed to silence the call before the phone rang a second time. Her mother was calling her. She'd call back immediately if Hannah wasn't careful. Her fingers fumbled for the *off* switch as she tried to power down the phone.

They heard the footsteps on the creaking beams in the attic above them, followed by the first man's voice.

"Did you hear that?"

"What?"

"Sounded like a phone," the first man said. "Check it out."

"I didn't hear anything."

The first man said something that neither Brian or Hannah could make out. The next thing they heard was the sound of someone climbing from the attic into the kitchen.

Hannah pointed to the hallway. Would they make it to the front door and out into the woods before he saw them?

It was too late. The footsteps were drawing closer. The man was coming for them. Brian looked around for something they could use to defend themselves, but anything that might be useful as a makeshift weapon was too far out of reach. If he made a move, he'd be seen. If he stayed where he was, they'd be found sooner rather than later. He didn't know what to do.

And then the man was in the room.

They heard a click, followed by another. On the third click they smelled smoke. The man had lit a cigarette. Although they didn't realize it, both of them were holding their breath.

The man crossed the floor as Brian and Hannah pressed themselves into the ground, trying to make themselves as invisible as possible. They knew it was ridiculous. They were caught. Once he took a step around the back of the couch, he'd see them.

They waited. And waited.

The couch sagged.

It took Brian a moment to realize the man was sitting on it. The lazy thief was sitting on the couch, smoking a cigarette. He wasn't looking for them at all.

"See anything?" came the voice from the attic.

"Not yet. I'm still looking around," the man said, exhaling a long, thin stream of acrid smoke. He stomped his feet on the ground to make it seem as if he was searching the house.

A long arm reached out over the back of the couch, the cigarette gripped between its fingers. The man tapped a column of ash from the cigarette. It dropped right onto Brian's face.

He thought he was going to sneeze. Hannah must have thought that, too, because a look of horror crossed her face. Somehow, Brian managed to restrain himself, and the moment passed.

Hannah breathed out as slowly and silently as she could. This was torture. One small noise, one glance over the back of the couch, and the man would see them.

But he never looked.

After what seemed like an eternity, he finished his cigarette and got to his feet.

"You must be hearing things," he shouted to his companion in the attic. "There's no sign of any mobile phone."

"Well, come back up and give me a hand, then. We need to get out of here."

Debra O'Loughlin had to hold Sam back to prevent him from rushing into the cottage. They'd walked through the woods together. At one point Debra thought she'd heard voices off to their left, but by the time she'd gotten the three youngsters to quiet down she couldn't hear anything any longer. Once they'd reached the clearing, it took her a couple of minutes to persuade Sam to remain behind an oak tree nearly ten yards farther back, where Amelia and Chris were already waiting. When she was certain he was going to stay put, she pushed the door of the cottage open. Even though she didn't expect to find any criminals running around, she still felt a prickle of nerves.

"Hello," she called out. "Anyone in there?"

There was no reply.

She stepped into the hallway and then into the living room. It was just as the three youngsters had described it.

"This is Officer Debra O'Loughlin of Newpark station. If there's anyone here, show yourself."

Her words lingered in the damp air for a moment before two heads slowly rose up from behind the couch. They belonged to Hannah Fitzgerald and Brian McDonnell. Officer O'Loughlin didn't think she'd ever seen such relieved faces in all her life.

Shortly afterward, when the Misfits met up again, was the moment Debra decided she never, ever wanted to have children. The screeching, the babbling, and the high-fiving was too much for her to take.

Hannah had snuck off to call her mother and reassure her that she was fine, telling her she'd dropped the phone when trying to answer it and that it had switched itself off, but was working perfectly now and that she'd be back home soon. Her mother sounded skeptical, but then she usually did when Hannah explained why her day hadn't followed the very neat path her parents had laid out for her.

As soon as she'd ended the call, Hannah joined Brian in begging Debra to chase after the criminals. They told her that two men had taken the stolen goods that had been hidden in the attic. Debra didn't know if they were making it up or if they really believed it, but she didn't see any sign of criminal activity.

"You're telling me you found some stolen items in the attic?"

"Yes," the Misfits chorused.

"Then three of you came to fetch me and report this alleged crime, while Brian and Hannah remained here."

"Yes."

"And the criminals chose that exact moment to take all of these stolen items away? While Brian and Hannah were stuck behind the couch the whole time and never got to see the men's faces?"

"That's exactly it," Hannah said.

"Right. It does seem a little far-fetched. Look, guys and girls, I know Newpark isn't the most exciting town in the world and when young people get together their imaginations can go into overdrive. I understand that. So I'm not sure this actually happened. At least, not in the way you believe. There's bound to be some innocent explanation for all this."

"We're not making it up. I don't have an imagination. I believe in logic, Debra. You know that. Please, have a look in the attic. They'll have left some clues," Chris said.

Unlike Brian, Debra had no difficulty in climbing into the attic. Her navy-uniformed legs dangled for a moment in midair, and then, with a grunt, she disappeared from view completely. She had told the others to wait downstairs. The last thing she needed was one of them falling through the ceiling. She could do without that hassle.

She shone her flashlight around the small space. The only thing out of the ordinary was a small hinged ledge near the peak of the roof. It could have been used to conceal some stolen goods, she supposed, but it was unlikely. In her experience, criminals made things easier for themselves rather than more difficult, and getting any stolen items in and out of these woods and in and out of an attic would be difficult.

"There's nothing here," she said.

"Nothing? They've taken it all?" Hannah cried. "Hang on, I'm coming up."

"No, no one else is coming up," Debra said. "Is that clear?"

Hannah's head popped up through the attic door.

"Oh, for crying out loud," Debra said.

A quick search later and Hannah was distraught.

"It's empty," she cried. "They've taken everything."

Debra just about managed to stop Sam from climbing up, too, finally ushered Hannah back down, and then took one last look around, just in case she'd missed anything. When she was satisfied that she hadn't, she dropped down into the kitchen and dusted herself off as five expectant young faces stared up at her.

"We have to move quickly to track them down. They could be anywhere in a few hours' time and our chance will have gone," Hannah said. "Can you put out an APB?"

"An APB is American," Debra said. "And I can't issue an arrest warrant when I don't suspect any crime has taken place."

"But we saw—" Brian began.

"It's gone. I can't believe it's all gone," Amelia said. She hadn't even seen the jewelry, and now she never would.

"You know what else is gone?" Debra said. "Me."

"Wait, you can't go yet. We know where the criminals are," Sam said.

"You do? Where?"

"Er, yes, Chris, where have they gone?" Sam asked.

"I don't know, but with Debra's help, we can find them," Chris said.

"Exactly, it's only been an hour, so they can't have gotten far. Let's go after them. We can put on the siren," Brian said.

"For the last time, there'll be no siren. I've already wasted enough time," Debra said. "I have to go back to the station."

Despite their pleadings and their certainty that they'd be able to catch the thieves in the act of transporting the goods, they couldn't persuade Debra to go after them.

Forlorn, they trudged through the woods until they emerged near Seamus Barry's farm, where Debra had parked the patrol car.

"What do you want me to do—spend my day driving around looking for them?" she asked as they drove back toward town. Four of the five were squashed into the back of the car, Sam's head hanging out of the window like a pet dog. Chris was in the passenger seat.

"No, of course not. We'll only crack this case through evidence," Chris said. "You need trackers, sniffer dogs, and a top-notch forensics team."

"That's a shame," Debra replied. "Today's their day off."

"All of them? Why would they all have the same day off? That's just extremely poor planning," Chris said.

"I think she's joking," Amelia said.

"I don't get it."

"Newpark doesn't have trackers, sniffer dogs, and a top-notch forensics team," Sam said, the wind rushing through his hair. "You'd know that if you weren't such a space cadet."

"Well, it should have those things. Maybe then we wouldn't have thieves running all over the place."

"Maybe so," Debra said.

Brian was furious that she was giving up so quickly. Maybe his dad had been right about the Newpark police force all along—he'd always said they were useless.

"I want all of you to stay well away from that cottage," Debra warned them.

"But—" Hannah began.

"No buts."

"But, if you don't think there's anyone sinister there, and the cottage is a safe place, then why do we need to stay away?" Hannah said.

"Didn't I just say 'no buts'?"

The expressions that stared back at her in the reflection of the rearview mirror were decidedly stony.

"Look," Debra continued, her voice a little softer. "I just want you to stay away from that place. It's not your property, so if you do go in there you're trespassing. I'm going to keep what happened today between us, but if I even think for one moment that you're considering going back, if I even *smell* the possibility of it, then I'll tell your parents."

Telling parents or guardians wasn't much of a threat as far as Brian and Amelia were concerned, but Debra O'Loughlin had thought of that, too.

"If Sam, Chris, and Hannah get into trouble, then they'll be grounded. That means no more Misfits."

Brian must have looked surprised because she directed her next comment at him.

"Yes, I've heard of the Misfits Club. I keep track of all the gangs around here. It's part of my job."

"Oh, we're not a gang, we're just a—" Amelia began.

Hannah laid her hand on Amelia's arm. "She's messing with you, Amelia."

"I'm not messing with you about going back to the woods, though. Stay clear. Okay?"

"Yes," they all said in unison.

The moment Debra had entered the station and closed the door behind her, Brian turned to the others.

"Right, how are we going to track those criminals down?" he asked.

WANTED PERSON

LAMBERT, ALEX

Wanted by the judicial authorities of the USA
for prosecution/to serve a sentence

IDENTITY PARTICULARS

PRESENT FAMILY NAME: Lambert
FIRST NAME: Alex
DATE OF BIRTH: 03/03/1972
PLACE OF BIRTH: Ireland
LANGUAGES SPOKEN: English, French

CHARGES

Grand larceny. Illegal import and export of goods.

IF YOU HAVE ANY INFORMATION, PLEASE CONTACT:
Your local police force
General Secretariat of Interpol

FOURTEEN

Brian could hardly believe it. His friends were turning into wimps right before his eyes. He knew Chris was a nervous character, but he'd always thought that he'd be one of those people who'd come through for you when it really counted, but, no, he was actually refusing to chase after the criminals. Brian was even more surprised at the others. Hannah had spent half her life with her head buried in detective novels and, now that she had the chance to solve a real mystery, she was running away from it. Where was their sense of adventure?

"Say it again, because I can't believe my ears," Brian said.

"We're not tracking them," Chris said.

"Speak for yourself," Sam said.

"We can't risk it. Debra's smart. She'll be keeping an eye on things and if she spots us acting suspiciously today, she'll definitely tell our parents and we can say good-bye to this investigation," Hannah said. "Being able to leave the house at some point in our lives is an important part of being able to find those guys."

"But we have to look for them now, don't we? They could

be in Zanzibar or Moscow or Lima by tonight," Amelia said.

"Thank you, Amelia," Brian said. He was really starting to warm to her. First the gummi snakes, now this. She'd only been an official member of the club for a few hours, yet she wasn't giving up like the rest of them.

"We'll find another way," Hannah said.

She checked the time on her phone. "Lunch first, then we'll work something out. Trust me."

Amelia did trust her. Hannah seemed smart. "Okay, I'll wait until after lunch, too," Amelia said.

"So, it's settled just like that?" Brian said. He was so frustrated he wanted to hit something. What was wrong with all of them? Didn't they care? This was their last adventure, their last time together. Could they not see how important this was? "Well, you all can stay at home eating and making plans, but I'm going out and I'm going to find those two. I'll do it by myself if I have to."

His belly rumbled, a great big rolling thunder of a sound.

"Are you hungry?" Amelia asked.

"That wasn't my stomach," he snapped. There was no time to be hungry, even though he was starving as usual.

It rumbled again, even louder this time. The other four looked at him.

"Okay, that one was me," he admitted.

"Want to come back to my grandmother's? She'll make

you something to eat. It'll make it easier for us all to meet up and decide our next move afterward," Amelia said.

"No, I don't. I want to do some detectivizing and I want to do it now."

"Might be better doing that on a full stomach. Brains are sharper when you're not hungry. Do you like old-fashioned food like bacon and cabbage and homemade soups and things like that?"

"I'll eat anything," Brian said. He was still angry, but what Amelia was promising sounded like just what he needed.

"Brian's got the constitution of an ox with a stomach made of cement," Chris said. "I once saw him eat four packets of chips and two packets of bitterly sour gummies just before he ate breakfast. And it wasn't a small breakfast, either."

Amelia tried her best not to look disgusted.

"I do like food," Brian said. "Maybe it wouldn't do any harm to have a quick bite before we get going again."

"We'll meet up at four p.m., at headquarters. That okay for everyone?" Hannah asked.

Brian had never spoken to Amelia's grandmother before. He'd seen her a few times when he'd been coming in or out of Hannah's house and she'd been at her gate, and he'd even waved to her once or twice, but he'd never spoken to her. She was a big bundle of a woman who always seemed ready to laugh.

"This isn't my first time seeing this young man," Amelia's grandmother said.

Now that he was standing close to her, Brian noticed how gray her hair was and that her face was both ruddy-cheeked and heavily lined.

"What's your name?" she asked.

"Brian."

"Brian? You don't look like a Brian to me. I think I'll call you Derek instead. My name is Florence, but you can call me Mrs. Parkinson."

Brian looked to Amelia, unsure of what to say or do.

"Is that all right with you, Derek?"

"Not really, Mrs. Parkinson. My name is Brian."

"He's got backbone. Good, good. You're not as terrible at making friends as I suspected, Amelia. Well done—first that Hannah girl, although her parents are exceptionally dull, and now Derek here. Progress is being made. Come in and make yourself at home."

The farmhouse kitchen was unlike any kitchen Brian had ever been in before. Pots of meat and vegetables bubbled on the black-and-white stove. Clothes were hung out to dry on makeshift lines that crisscrossed the room, including some giant underpants that made Brian blush and turn away when he realized that they probably belonged to Florence. Dishes that needed a wash were piled in the sink. The place was messy and cluttered, but even though he was normally tidy himself he liked it.

Although she looked strong and clumpy, Florence Parkinson was light on her feet. She almost floated across the kitchen. She took a wooden spoon and began to stir something that bubbled in a large silver pot, something that Brian thought smelled absolutely delicious.

"It's stew again, I'm afraid," Gran said. "Do you like stew, Derek?"

"Brian. Yes, I love it."

"Fabulous. You're not one of those picky eaters, then? Not like my darling granddaughter. She has to know the ingredients in everything before she'll consider trying it. Is this organic, Gran? Well, it's been grown in a field, Amelia, and fertilized with cow sh—"

"What have you been up to this morning, Gran?" Amelia interrupted.

"This'n'that, this'n'that. Right, you two, wash your paws and we'll eat."

Amelia picked out some of the dishes from the sink and placed them on the draining board. Both Brian and Amelia leaned into the sink at the same time to wash their hands. Amelia turned on the tap then passed the red bar of carbolic soap to Brian.

"You get used to the smell," she said, referring to the soap.

"It smells like the stuff you put on your leg when you get a cut," Brian said.

"You'll find a lot of things in Gran's house that you won't find in other people's," she said.

Their conversation was interrupted by the bleating of a lamb.

"Shoo, Richard Hannay, shoo," Gran said.

A little black lamb had click-clacked into the kitchen without anyone noticing. Brian watched, amazed, as Amelia's grandmother ushered him out again, flapping a tea towel at his hindquarters as the little guy scampered back outside.

"You're nothing but a pest, Richard Hannay," she said, pulling the back door shut, although she said it in such a way that Brian knew she liked him.

"His mother died and Gran raised him herself. He's sort of adapted to being with the flock now, but every so often he wanders back into the kitchen to nose around."

"Why is he called Richard Hannay?"

"I think it's from a movie or something. Gran calls all the animals after characters from movies and books."

"Your grandmother is . . ." Brian began, not quite finding the right words to finish the sentence.

"She's nothing like my dad—he's her son. Dad likes everything neat and tidy and just so, but Gran, well, everything's all messy and topsy-turvy with her. You never know what's going to happen next."

Brian quite liked that. Especially when what happened next was a superb lunch. It tasted every bit as good as it had smelled and he relished every bite. He normally didn't eat vegetables since his father had such a hatred of them, but he loved these—fresh parsnips and carrots and peas and onions. He decided he'd happily go to Florence's for lunch every day of the week. Unlike Brian, Amelia picked at her food, pushing it around her plate. She'd barely eaten half of it by the time her grandmother had started to clear up.

"Right, you two, you've had your lunch, now it's time to pay for your meal."

Brian looked worried. "I don't have any money on me right now. I—"

"Oh, Derek, you are a funny little fella. I'm not expecting you to pay with money. I'm expecting you to pay with manual labor."

Florence needed them to help her fix a broken fence that was threatening to fall down and let her small flock of sheep roam free. She gave Brian a pair of tattered navy overalls that were a couple of sizes too big for him. He had to roll up the sleeves and legs so he could move around. Even though he didn't mind wearing his own sneakers, Florence wouldn't hear of it. She gave him one of her spare pairs of rain boots; they were a pale pink and covered in bright blue polka dots.

"I'm not wearing those," he spluttered when he saw them.

"Why ever not?" Florence asked.

"They're girls' boots."

"Nonsense, they're just a little colorful—that's all," she replied. She looked down at her own black pair, streaked with muck. "Although, I have to admit, I prefer these. The pair you're wearing were a present. More a fashion statement than a working pair of rain boots. Whoever bought them for me doesn't know much about rain boots or farm life."

"I bought them for you," Amelia pouted.

Florence broke into great peals of laughter. "I really put my foot in it there, didn't I?" she said, giving her granddaughter a friendly shove. "Right, Derek, if you're brave enough to wear them, then you can come for lunch tomorrow as well."

That was enough for Brian. He hated rain boots, but he loved Florence's cooking.

"I look ridiculous," he said, minutes later, as they tramped through the field.

If he was hoping Amelia would reassure him that he didn't actually look ridiculous, it was a false hope. She kept snickering at him. When she wasn't snickering, she was taking photos with her phone, photos she was planning to show to the others later on. The grumpier Brian grew, the more delighted she became. The boots weren't just too colorful, they were a little too big as well, something that Florence had remedied by crumpling up some newspaper and stuffing it in the toe of each boot.

"You're a bit short for your age, aren't you?" she said, although not unkindly.

Brian's sense of ridiculousness was made worse by Amelia's stylishness. She looked as if she was heading for a fashion show rather than a couple of hours' work in the field.

Brian soon found out that physical work wasn't as bad as his father made out. In fact, he quite enjoyed it. Brian held the fence posts in place while Florence hammered them into the doughy earth with a huge sledgehammer. Then they tacked the silver-colored mesh wire to the post.

Amelia did her best to help, but she was more of a hindrance and was annoyed with herself when she kept making silly mistakes. She couldn't understand how she was able to do so well in school, always near the top of her class, yet doing something like putting up a fence made her look foolish. She fell over twice, somehow managed to staple her second-favorite cardigan to a post, and was finally persuaded to take a break when, after insisting she could control the sledgehammer, she almost smashed Brian's toes. Luckily, she hit the part of the boot that was filled with crumpled paper.

"I'm not normally this soft with her," Florence whispered when Amelia was engrossed in posting a picture of them working online. "But she's finding it difficult now, having to move out of her own home because of all the fights and the baby stuff. It's a big change."

Brian didn't know what to say, so he just nodded. He thought Amelia had said she was here for a few weeks to look after her grandmother. He didn't think he'd ever met anybody who needed less looking after than Florence

Parkinson. And what was all that about the baby stuff and having to move out? He wondered why Amelia had told him differently.

Florence smiled. "You're a good worker."

"Thanks," he said.

He'd enjoyed the work. Really enjoyed it. And, to his surprise, he found he liked the praise, too. It made him feel all warm and sort of glowy inside, not that he'd tell anyone that.

By the time they'd finished and washed up and Amelia had changed outfits—from her farm-working clothes into a print sweatshirt and skinny jeans—it was a few minutes past four o'clock. They were late meeting the others in the den.

Chris stood up. He had a blue folder in his hand. He opened it and handed a printout to each of them. It was the picture Amelia had taken at the cottage, the one he'd enlarged the previous day.

"We have to find out who this person is," Hannah said. "I think he's the guy in charge of the stolen goods and I believe he has at least one man, maybe two working for him. One of them seems to be lazy and he smokes. The other seems to want to do his job properly."

"They might have already left the country or at least gone somewhere that's difficult for us to find them," Chris said.

"Like Zanzibar," Amelia said.

"Yes, Amelia, like Zanzibar."

"We're not going to be able to search for them anywhere that isn't within cycling distance of Newpark," Brian said.

"I know, but we have to assume they're still in the area. Just because they moved the goods, it doesn't mean they've moved them very far. They might be just driving around . . ." Hannah said.

For a moment, it looked as if there was something wrong with Brian. He shut his eyes and lay back on a beanbag without saying a word. Amelia guessed he had some kind of headache, but she was wrong.

"Are you okay?" she asked.

He put a finger to his lips to ask for silence. He needed to think. Driving around, Hannah had said. Mrs. Doherty, the shopkeeper, hadn't recognized the two men who'd been in the Subaru Impreza. She'd thought they were just driving around, too.

It was coming back to him now. He hadn't recognized the voices in the cottage immediately because when he'd heard them previously—other than when they'd been roaring threats at him—he'd been groggy after his fall. They'd sounded slightly different then, a little blurry, if a sound could be blurry. That's why it had taken him a while to remember. But it was them, all right. He was sure of it. His eyes snapped open, like a villain suddenly coming back to life at the end of a movie.

"Nice creepy vibe," Sam said.

"The two men in the cottage drive a Subaru Impreza," Brian said.

"Wow, those were some really impressive Sherlock Holmes–type deductions there," Chris said. "How do you know? Paint flecks from the car on their clothing? One of them carrying a distinctive key fob that only works on that type of car? Something else from the mind palace?"

"No," Brian said. "I saw them driving it."

He explained what had happened to him when he'd encountered the men at Mrs. Doherty's shop. Sam was annoyed that Brian hadn't told them the story before, seeing as how their days were normally lacking in adventure, but he was shushed by the others. Brian told them everything he remembered about the situation.

"This gets more and more interesting," Hannah said.

Sam rolled his eyes. Anytime Hannah grew excited by a case, she said things were getting interesting.

"Have you ever seen them around Newpark before?" she asked.

"Never," Brian said. Unfortunately, he wasn't able to remember the car's license plate number, but Hannah reckoned they had enough information to get started.

Chris took note of the descriptions of the men. He was planning to find an online police sketch program later, but, to his surprise, Amelia volunteered her services as an artist. She explained that she spent some of her free time sketching and painting. She'd never shown her friends at home any of her work or even told them she drew. Somehow, she felt more comfortable around her new friends than she did with her friends back home.

Hannah gave her a pencil and paper, and Amelia got to work. Her skill as an artist was impressive, but her attempts to re-create the men's faces took longer than necessary due to Brian's inability to describe them clearly.

"He had a fatter head."

"Wider? More jowly? Chubbier cheeks?"

"Just fatter. Make it fatter."

"How exactly? You're not making sense."

"Put more fat on his head."

Finally, he was happy with the likenesses Amelia produced.

"Yes, that's them. It's actually really like them. That's great, Amelia."

"Shut up," Amelia muttered, embarrassed but pleased.

"We have to come up with a strategy," Chris said.

"Of course we do," Sam said. "We should color code it and print it out and laminate it and give it a sensible name."

Chris ignored the sarcasm. He unrolled the poster of the man in the woods. He looked a little like one of the men Amelia had drawn, but it was difficult to be sure.

The Misfits Club now knew what at least two of the men they were searching for looked like. They just had no idea how to find them.

PROGRESS REPORT ON THE CASE OF
THE COTTAGE IN THE WOODS
By Hannah Fitzgerald

It's been four days since we uncovered the treasure in the so-called Cottage in the Woods case and
progress has been slow and very frustrating. We
were warned not to go near the cottage again by the
twins' police-officer cousin, Debra, but Brian ignored
her warning—and ours—and decided to go back to the
woods by himself. He found no signs of life and no
other evidence, apart from a discarded cigarette butt
approximately twenty yards from the cottage entrance.
He put it in a plastic ziplock bag, just like I told him
to do with any evidence he found. Brian said he will
keep checking, but we believe that the men will no
longer be using this building to hide what they've
stolen. We just hope that they haven't disposed of
the items yet.

After a lot of talking, we came up with a plan.
Each club member was assigned a task, which I
have outlined in the rest of this official report.
Amelia and I spent hours working on an evidence
board, like the ones you see on detective shows. We
got some corkboard and pinned up the pictures of
the men, then we filled up index cards with all the

information we have so far—not that much—and our plan of action.

Mom caught us with it once, but we pretended we were using it as an ideas board to write our own detective story. She believed us. The only problem is she thought that it was a really fun thing to do and she wants to read our story when it's finished, so now we have to write one!

Amelia and I really enjoyed making the evidence board. I haven't told the boys yet, but she's my new best friend. Unlike the boys (well, Brian and Sam really), she doesn't find breaking wind, talking about vomit, or ridiculous pranks funny. She's great!

Sam has spent the whole time wandering around the town looking for the men. He has varied the time of day he visits in order to increase his chances of seeing them, but he hasn't had any luck so far. Part of the problem is that, although we have drawings of the men and a blurry photo, we can't show them to any adults in case they blab to our parents. If they did, the investigation would be ended immediately. I can guarantee that.

We knew Sam's chances of finding any of the suspects this way were very slim, but he was still really enthusiastic, especially in the beginning. He thought he'd found at least one of the men on six separate occasions, but each one turned out to be a false alarm. There was a little bit of trouble when he tried to perform a citizen's arrest on a suspect, but the misunderstanding was sorted out before it became too serious and the woman he'd mistaken for one of the criminals was kind enough not to take the matter further once Sam had apologized about seventeen times.

Sam was accompanied some of the time by Amelia, and by Brian at other times. Brian spoke to Mrs. Doherty, the shop owner who the two men had tried to steal from, but she was unable to provide us with any new information. Her shop doesn't have CCTV, so we were unable to obtain footage of either the men or the car. We'd hoped we might be able to get the license-plate number, but no such luck. She was one of the few people we showed the pictures to, since Brian trusted her, but although she confirmed that the drawings were accurate she wasn't able to be more helpful than that.

Chris has spent nearly all his free time researching stuff on the laptop. I have, too. We have both been looking to identify the items we spotted in the cottage—the painting, the jewelry, the lamp. We searched through tons of newspaper reports of burglaries and all kinds of thefts, but we couldn't find any mention of the items Sam and I had seen in the attic.

I'd hoped that we might find a photo of the painting of the ship online, but after hours of searching for it I still haven't found it. I think my eyes have dried up from staring at the screen for so long. Amelia made drawings of all the stolen goods, including the painting, based on my memories of it, and we've shown it to a number of people, like Déirdre Ní Laocha, a local artist, to see if they recognized it. Still nothing! I've found a website that does some kind of art analysis, but it's not free, so I'll have to sneak onto Dad's computer as he has all the credit card payment stuff set up on it.

When I'm not looking at the laptop, I've been rereading all of my mystery books, hoping to find something in there—an approach I haven't tried or a different way of thinking, anything that might help. I've read everything from The Sisters Grimm to Agatha Christie to The Westing Game. It hasn't produced any results yet, but it did get me into a crime-solving mood. There's a definite sprinkling of mystery in the air now, and I love it.

Brian has spent a lot of time biking around looking for the Subaru Impreza, as it's an easily recognizable car. He was certain he'd heard its distinctive engine once and raced down some alleys and side streets, almost colliding with a moving wheeled trash can, but by the time he'd reached the road there was no sign of it.

The whole process has been extremely frustrating, especially when we started out with such high hopes. We are not giving up, though—far from it. You can't just give up because something's a bit difficult. That'd be pathetic. But after days of hard work and no real reward, there have been some grumblings from the group. It's also been difficult to keep my parents off our backs. The amount of times they've almost overheard our discussions has been ridiculous. There have been far too many close calls to mention. It'd be much easier if we could meet elsewhere, but they don't monitor me as much if we're around my house, so it makes more sense to stay in headquarters.

Why can't we find anything? The men cannot just have disappeared, can they? There must be a clue or a piece of evidence. Something to give us hope. We can't keep going and going unless we have hope. The twins will be moving soon—their parents have already started packing some stuff away—so we don't have much time if we're going to solve the case before the Misfits Club is finished.

We need a breakthrough and we need it soon.

FIFTEEN

Brian, Mucky, and Mucky's girlfriend, Sharon, were in very bad moods, but not all for the same reason. Brian was annoyed that the investigation hadn't been progressing very well. It had been almost a week since they'd been in the cottage with the stolen goods and despite spending every minute of the day looking for the two men in the Subaru Impreza, he'd had no luck. It was as if they'd vanished from the face of the earth.

Mucky and Sharon (who'd been a more frequent visitor to the house recently) were in bad moods because of a party invitation. The Adamus, Chris and Sam's parents, had organized a going-away party and Mucky and Sharon had been invited. The party was that night, even though the family wasn't moving for another week. Mrs. Adamu reckoned they'd have enough to be organizing without having to add a party to the mix.

"Why do I have to go?" Mucky whined. "I don't like parties. All that having to talk to people and pretending you're interested in their boring lives. It's not for me, Shar."

"I want to go," Sharon said, with an air of finality that Mucky foolishly ignored.

"I'm not stopping you from going. I'd be delighted if you went. Nothing would make me happier than knowing you're having a good time. I just don't want to be beside you when you're having it."

"You're going, Mucky McDonnell, and you're going to dress up for it, too. No T-shirts," Sharon said. She slammed a mug on the table and the handle broke off.

Mucky and Brian exchanged worried glances, but neither said anything.

"I'm sorry," Sharon said. She massaged her temples. "We're going to the party because I need a night out. Work has been stressful lately. Things haven't been going as smoothly as I hoped and I need a break."

Brian still wasn't sure what Sharon did for a living, but he was smart enough to know that now wasn't the right time to ask.

"I'm going to take a nap. Make me a cup of tea, Mucky. And put that broken mug in the garbage."

She disappeared upstairs.

"This is all your fault," Mucky said when he was sure Sharon was out of earshot.

"My fault?"

"It's your friends that are leaving, not mine. We're only being invited because of you. So, thanks to you, I have to spend tonight bored out of my skull."

Brian had had enough. He couldn't take it anymore. "You're right, Dad. They are my friends—two of my best friends—and they're leaving, and all you care about is being bored for a couple of hours. You don't care how I feel about it, do you?"

"Of course I care," Mucky mumbled. He was taken aback by the flash of anger in his son's eyes. Brian had never spoken to him like that before.

"*Why* do you care?" Brian asked.

"I . . . um . . . because it makes you . . . sad? And that's . . . bad," Mucky said.

He really wasn't one for all this emotional stuff. If you didn't allow yourself to have emotions, then nothing could ever hurt you.

"Sad and bad. Brilliant, Dad, just brilliant. Do you even know my friends' names?"

"Yes," Mucky said.

"What are they?"

Mucky wasn't prepared for a follow-up question. "I want to say . . . Steve . . . and Paul?"

"I'm going out," Brian said.

He slammed the front door behind him, leaving Mucky alone downstairs. Brian's father sighed. All he wanted was a quiet, peaceful life and look what he had instead: a girlfriend he was a little bit intimidated by, and an ungrateful son.

A few minutes later, he'd forgotten about Sharon's anger, but the upset face of his son nagged at him a lot longer than he would have liked or expected.

SIXTEEN

Even though the day was bathed in warm sunshine, the Burger Joint in the center of Newpark was packed. Brian recognized some people from his school—Samantha and Ethan, a few of the crowd from Analeentha, including JJ, Luke, and Willow—a few others whose names he didn't know. He joined his four friends at their table, which was covered in empty burger wrappers and a few stray cold fries. A big fat folder of investigation notes that Chris had brought along was teetering on the edge of the table. The rest of the Misfits Club wasn't in much better spirits than Brian was.

"We've been at this forever and we're no closer to finding the men or the stolen goods. It's like looking for a needle in a haystack," Hannah said.

"It sure is," Amelia agreed.

Brian noticed that Amelia and Hannah seemed to agree on everything now.

"We need a magnet," Brian said. "If you want to find a needle in a haystack, you use a powerful magnet. We need a powerful magnet."

"Are we the needle or the haystack?" Sam asked.

Hannah sighed. "Neither. The guys in the pictures, the ones we're looking for, they're the needles, the entire world is the haystack."

"So, we're the magnet?" Sam said.

"No, the magnet is what we need to find them. It could be anything. We just haven't figured out what it is yet."

"This is all unclear. So, what are we?"

"We're still us," Hannah said.

"They're needles, the world's a haystack, but we're still us? None of this makes sense."

"Please shut up, Sam," Brian said. "You're wrecking my head."

This wasn't just his bad mood from his argument with his father. Brian had grown increasingly testy over the last few days. Several times, he'd said things like this to Sam, almost as if he was trying to start a fight. After all, it'd be harder to miss someone who was moving away if you weren't getting along with them. But Sam didn't respond to any of his taunts, which only made Brian feel worse.

"Sorry," he said.

"For what?" Sam grinned. "I do wreck people's heads. It's my thing. Sometimes, I even wreck my own head."

"What do we do now, Chris?" Amelia said.

She had grown more confident with the group the more she'd gotten to know them and had finally felt completely part of things when she'd called Brian a "woolly-headed muppet" without thinking when he'd made a ridiculous suggestion. The others had cracked up laughing and something clicked in her at that moment. She'd always felt welcome in the club, and had grown close to Hannah, but with that unthinking insult she realized again that she was more comfortable with them now than she ever had been with her own friends.

"The cottage in the woods has to be owned by somebody. If we find out who that is, then we'll find a link to the thieves. I'm certain of it," Chris said.

"Yes, we know that," Hannah said. "We've been trying to make that link for days, but it's been impossible to discover who the owner is. You've searched; I've searched. We've got nothing."

"Pssst."

At first no one heard the sound since it was drowned out by the tables of excited conversations taking place in the Burger Joint.

"PSSSST."

Amelia was the first to notice. She nudged Hannah. "There's a small, strange man looking at us," she whispered.

The man was somewhere between four and four and a half feet tall, wore sunglasses that were too big for his face, a fedora that was too large for his head, and a thick quilted jacket, which must have been extremely uncomfortable on such a warm day.

"That's not a small, strange man, that's a small, strange boy," Hannah said with a smile. "Hello, Horace."

Horace McCarthy edged closer to the table. He removed his sunglasses.

"Hi, guys, it's me, Horace."

"We figured that out. What's with the—"

"Disguise? I'm keeping a low profile. The last thing I want is to renew acquaintance with Smasher. I don't think that'd end well for me."

"I'm sure he's forgotten all about it," Chris said. "He probably bullies people on a daily basis. He'd need a database to keep track of everyone he has to beat up."

"I'm not taking any chances. This is my first time out of the house in days. Thought I'd grab a burger," Horace squeaked. "Anyway, that's not why I'm here. I couldn't help overhearing your predicament."

"Our predicament?" Brian said.

"Yes, Misfits business. I'm not going to lie—I was eavesdropping. Always been a fan of clubs and investigations and things like that. Also, I owe you one for saving my life."

"Sorry, Horace," Sam said. "I don't understand a word you're saying."

"You're looking for information on who owns a property, right? I can help you. My dad knows who owns every house in town. Before he ran the gift shop, he was a real estate agent."

The Misfits were back in their club headquarters an hour later, sitting on their comfortable beanbags, pages of investigation notes scattered on the rug in front of them. Brian and Sam were sharing a bag of chips and Amelia was flipping through the pages of some of Hannah's mystery novels when Chris's phone rang. He went outside, paced up and down the garden path for a minute, deep in conversation, before ending the call and returning to the shed.

"That was Horace. His father told him that the cottage in the woods belongs to a Mr. Rodney O'Reilly," he said.

Four faces looked blankly at him.

"Are we supposed to know who that is?" Brian asked.

"Oh, I kind of thought you would know," Chris said. His words hadn't had the impact he'd expected them to have.

"Rodney O'Reilly," he repeated, although the repetition of the man's name didn't make things any clearer. "Ranting Rodney."

"Ohhh, him. I remember him," Sam said.

"Of course you do. He's only shouted at you about twenty different times. He said you were an idiot."

"He said I was a *thundering* idiot," Sam said, almost proudly.

Recognition slowly dawned on Brian's and Hannah's faces, too, as Chris explained to Amelia who Ranting Rodney O'Reilly was. He was a local man who was well-known for his fits of rage. Rodney would get into a furious temper over the most minor inconvenience or perceived slight.

He lived in the heart of the town on a narrow street

where the front doors of the houses opened out onto the sidewalk. This meant that occasionally passersby would stop outside his front door to take a phone call or tie their shoelaces. They'd soon realize that this was a mistake when the door swung open and they received a verbal volley of abuse from Rodney for the crime of momentarily loitering outside his house. His list of intolerances was quite lengthy, including, but not limited to: talking too loudly, talking too quietly, fidgeting, looking the wrong way at him, coughing, sneezing, and breathing too noisily. He was one of Newpark's most unpleasant characters.

"I wouldn't have thought that Rodney was the kind of person who'd own a cottage. His house is tiny and my dad always said if he'd been busy working rather than sitting at home he wouldn't spend so much time ranting," Hannah said.

"He inherited it from an uncle who died. It's not worth much since nobody wanted to live out there, but someone might pay him for the use of it," Chris said.

"The bad guys," Brian said. "The bad guys are renting it from him and storing their stuff there."

"If they are, then Rodney must know them. He might be the key to finding them, or at least finding out who they are," Hannah said. "This just got interesting."

"So what do we do now?" Sam asked.

"We pay Rodney a visit," Hannah said.

Of course, that wasn't what Hannah told her mother.

She said they were going for a bike ride, which was partly true, since it was too far for them to walk to Rodney's house. While Hannah got ready, the other four waited outside in the yard.

They'd spent some of the ten minutes they'd been waiting mocking Amelia's bike, which was a solid old thing that belonged to her grandmother. Florence had kept it in almost perfect condition over the years and, despite what the boys said, Amelia thought it was very stylish.

"What are we going to say to Rodney?" Amelia asked, trying to change the subject.

"Leave it to me," Sam said. "I'll do all the talking, because I'm naturally charming."

"You really believe that, don't you?" Brian said.

"You've either got it or you don't, and I've got it," Sam said.

Amelia's jaw dropped open, not in response to Sam's unnatural confidence, rather because she'd just seen Hannah emerge from her house.

"Anyone says a word, I break their face," Hannah said when she joined them at the gate.

The others struggled not to smile.

Hannah was wearing a luminous green bicycle helmet and a luminous yellow safety vest over her shirt, as well as a pair of reflective sunglasses. There were elastic pads on her elbows, knees, and ankles. A whistle, to call for help in case of emergency, hung around her neck. And the bicycle itself had two bells and a mirror. All it was missing from a safety point of view were stabilizers on the back wheels.

"Have you got your phone with you, Hannah?" Mr. Fitzgerald shouted from the front door.

"Yes, Daddy," Hannah called back. "And it's fully charged."

"Be careful and don't forget to check in with me. I love you."

"I love you, too," Hannah said sweetly. She lowered her voice and muttered to the others. "I mean it—one word and faces will be broken."

They cycled through the front gate, Sam leading the way. "You look good, Hannah," Brian said, barely getting the words out before he started laughing.

"You're first on my list, McDonnell," Hannah said. "When you least expect it, that's when I'll strike."

The ride into town was uneventful. They found Rodney's little house on a narrow side street. It was as small as Hannah had said. The curtains were drawn and there wasn't any sign of life. Hannah rang the doorbell and when that received no response Sam pounded on the door with his fist for a full minute. There was still no reply.

"Hey."

The shout came from the house next door. A disheveled head peered out from an upstairs window.

"Hello there," Chris said.

"Don't 'hello there' me. What's all that racket about? Don't you know what time it is?"

"Yes, it's four o'clock."

"In the afternoon?"

"Yeah."

"Oh. That's not so bad. Must have lost track of the time. What do you want?"

The man told them that Rodney had moved out some time back. He'd been transferred to Merlehan's Nursing Home. A quick Google search on Chris's phone revealed the location and that the visiting hours were between two and five o'clock. It was less than two miles away. They'd have time to make it.

WILD FRIENDS' FEDERATION

15 Elsinore Avenue | Lambeth | London SE1 7UQ

Chris Adamu

104 College Wood

Newpark

Dear Chris,

Many thanks for sending WFF the money you raised from your school bake sale. Well done on raising €175.23. It's an impressive achievement! Please pass on our thanks to all those who bought the cakes to help our cause.

I know it is difficult to raise money, but every penny you send us goes toward helping the welfare of wild animals. Without this care, many of them would not survive.

We would also like to thank you for pledging to donate fifty percent of your pocket money to our federation. You are extremely generous. Your efforts on behalf of the animals and the environment are appreciated and very welcome.

With kind regards,

Jack Adams

Jack Adams

SEVENTEEN

The nursing home was tucked away at the end of a cul-de-sac none of them had ever been down before. It was far larger than any of them would have guessed and Amelia thought it resembled a small school or hospital. The parking lot was almost full. They biked over to the grass median, climbed off their bikes, and laid them on their sides on the grass. Chris decided to stay with the bikes since none of them had brought locks with them and he was worried they might be stolen.

"No one's going to take them," Brian said, but Chris couldn't be convinced otherwise.

"Just because you don't think they'll be stolen, doesn't mean they won't," he said.

"Hannah, give him your whistle. That way, if a group of bike-stealing mega thugs arrives on the scene, he can attract our attention," Sam said.

"One long peep on the whistle if it's potential danger, three peeps if it's the gravest danger," Amelia said.

Chris took a pad of paper and a pen from his backpack,

which was always filled with items he considered useful for adventuring, and handed them to Amelia.

"You'll need that for your cover story," he said.

A set of double doors led into the nursing home. They didn't open automatically as they approached, so Sam began pushing and pulling at the handles until Amelia pointed to the sign that read: *Press doorbell and wait for admission.*

"Must be some kind of security measure," Brian said.

Sam straightened up as Hannah pressed the doorbell.

"Well, that made me look like a dope," he said good-naturedly.

"If it's any consolation, we already knew you were a dope," Hannah said.

The receptionist buzzed them in.

There were several old people sitting in armchairs and wheelchairs in the neutral-colored lobby of the nursing home. Some of them were dressed in sweaters and tracksuit pants with elastic waists, while others were in dressing gowns and pajamas. There were potted plants everywhere and a small brown-and-white terrier lay asleep in the corner.

"Good afternoon," the receptionist said cheerily. "Can I help you?"

"We're here to see Rodney O'Reilly," Sam said. "He's not expecting us and we haven't made an appointment or anything. We're here to do a school summer project on local characters and everyone knows Rodney."

That's what Chris had told them to say. It worked like a treat, too.

"Oh, that sounds great. Rodney doesn't get too many visitors. Some people aren't able to deal with his . . . um . . . robust views on the world."

The receptionist asked a nurse to show the others to the television room where Rodney and some of the residents were glued to daytime TV. Rodney was a well-built man who was barely contained by his chair. Brian thought he looked like a retired wrestler.

"Rodney, you have some visitors," the nurse said.

Rodney took one look at the new arrivals. "Don't like them," he grunted. If Rodney recognized Sam, he didn't show any sign of it. He'd ranted at so many people in his life that every time he met someone he assumed he'd either shouted at them before, or that he'd be shouting at them soon.

The nurse rolled her eyes, as if she'd heard this from him a hundred times before. He was a man who'd gone through life never liking anything or anyone. The only times he'd ever been truly happy were when he'd seen somebody fall over or make a fool of themselves in some way.

"Sorry about that," the nurse said to the Misfits, "but if he doesn't want to talk to you—"

"When did I say that, you fool of a girl?" Rodney snapped. "I don't like them, but that doesn't mean I don't want to talk to them. Better than talking to the rest of the brain-dead inmates. Or, if not better, at least it'll be a change. You, Big Nose, bring over some of the empty armchairs. Yes, I'm talking to you."

Nobody had ever told Brian he had a big nose before. He didn't think so.

"Well, aren't you a delight," Sam muttered.

"What was that?"

"I was just saying that the chairs are light. I thought they'd be heavier."

They dragged four armchairs—which actually *were* heavy—across the carpet and arranged them in a semicircle around Rodney. The nurse made her excuses and left, glad to escape from the old man and his cantankerous ways.

"You're an odd-looking bunch," Rodney said.

"It's a pleasure to meet you, too," Hannah said.

"Don't try sarcasm on me, kid. I invented sarcasm and I'm immune to it. Now, what do you want?"

"We're doing a school project—" Amelia began.

"School's for losers. Nothing worth learning can be learned in school. Teachers are just people who are too scared to go out and get a real job," Rodney said, shifting around in the armchair, trying to get comfortable.

His voice was loud and carried around the room, drowning out whatever withering comment the talk show host was delivering onscreen. A couple of the residents looked around, annoyed at the interruption to their television-watching.

"What are you guys looking at?" Rodney asked them.

Nobody replied. It wasn't worth getting on the wrong side of him. He'd just make their lives miserable.

"Bunch of tulips," Rodney said, turning back to the Misfits. "What do you want to know about me for?"

"We have a school summer project where we're supposed to do a short biography of an interesting character in our town and our parents said that Rodney O'Reilly is one of Newpark's most important characters of the last fifty years."

"Did they now? First of all, it's Mr. Rodney O'Reilly," Rodney said, correcting her. "And, secondly, don't think flattery's going to work on me."

It did work, though, because he let them ask him some questions about life in the town over the years, what it had been like in the 1950s and what his favorite memories were from that time. It turned out that Rodney didn't like anything about that time or anybody he'd encountered in his day-to-day life. In fact, it soon transpired that he didn't like anything at all, although he did like complaining about what he disliked. He liked that a lot.

Amelia pretended to take notes as he ranted and raved about many different aspects of life in a very random order, including: Elvis Presley, "a talentless fraud with enough grease in his hair to fry French fries"; soccer, "a game for simpletons with the IQ of a slow amoeba"; politics, "only an imbecile would vote for any eejit stupid enough to want to be in government"; and plenty more. Any guilt the four visitors felt at tricking Rodney disappeared somewhere around the middle of this twenty-minute rage against the world. Amelia didn't think she'd ever met a more unpleasant person in her whole life. In the end, when Brian felt as if his ears were about to bleed, Hannah managed to steer the conversation away from Rodney's hatred of everything, and toward the topic they'd come here to ask him about.

"So, Mr. O'Reilly, you've lived in the same house all your life?"

"I'm a proud Newparker, born and bred. Why would I ever want to move?" Rodney said with a belch and a wiggle of his wild thatch of eyebrows.

"To travel a bit and see the world?" Amelia suggested.

"Travel? What's traveling except going from one place to another place and then going back to where you started from? Waste of time," Rodney said. "Turn on the TV and you can see the rest of the world if you're into that kind of nonsense."

"You've never wanted to live anywhere else? Never thought of buying a vacation home, or, y'know, a place in the country?" Hannah said.

"No," he said. "Never thought of it. I'm a townie through and through."

"Funny you should mention a place in the country. A

friend of my dad's is looking to rent a small cottage, but he can't find any," Sam said.

"What's that got to do with me?" Rodney barked. "Do I look like a real estate agent?"

The gang didn't know Rodney well enough to interpret the change in his expression. There was a glint of suspicion in his eyes. Sam, however, did know Hannah well enough to interpret the angry look on her face. He shouldn't have mentioned the cottage. Not yet.

Rodney looked at them for a moment before he slowly stood up, wobbling briefly before steadying himself on the arm of his chair. Brian moved to help him, but Rodney's glare was enough to tell him to back off.

"I have to pee," he said. "I'll be back soon. When you get to my age, you have to pee every five minutes."

"Thanks for the information," Sam muttered.

Rodney towered over them, looking from one face to the other, before he lumbered off in the direction of the toilets. He pushed through the swinging doors that led to the hallway, then glanced back to make sure none of the Misfits were following him. When he was certain they weren't, he took a mobile phone with a large screen and a huge keypad from his bathrobe pocket and dialed a number.

"Which one are you? Lionel or Burt? Don't answer. It doesn't matter. I think you've got trouble. Bunch of kids have arrived and they're asking some weird questions," Rodney said.

"Keep them there. We're on our way," Lionel or Burt replied.

As soon as Rodney arrived back in the television room and settled into his armchair, Hannah knew something was wrong.

"It's been really nice having some visitors. I love chatting," Rodney said. He tried to smile, but it came out all wrong, as if he hadn't smiled in forty years. His face was twisted and bordering on gruesome.

"It's been great to talk to you, too. You've really helped us a lot. I'm sure we'll get an A for our school project," Hannah said warily.

"Definitely. There's some top-notch stuff there," Brian said.

"What did you say your names were again?" Rodney asked.

"Didn't we tell you?" Hannah said.

"No, you told me very little about yourselves."

"Well, that was rude. I'm so sorry we forgot to introduce ourselves, Mr. O'Reilly," Hannah said.

Silence hung in the air.

"You still haven't told me your names," Rodney said, leaning forward a little menacingly. A cold shudder ran down Amelia's spine.

"He's Julian, that's Dick, that's Anne, and I'm George—it's short for Georgina," Hannah said. "Timmy's waiting outside."

"They're lovely names," Rodney said, continuing his grim attempt at a smile. "Do you live nearby?"

"Yes. Do you know the apartments near Shortcastle?"

Rodney nodded that he did.

"Well, we're all from there. That's how we got to know each other," Hannah lied.

Amelia had picked up on Hannah's suspicions and grew even more uncomfortable. She didn't like this man and didn't want to remain in his company any longer.

"We'd better be going," Amelia said, rising from her armchair.

"No, don't go yet," Rodney said. "Stay for a cup of tea. I don't get many visitors, and you're hardly going to up and leave now after I've spent all this time helping you with your project, are you?"

"Of course not," Hannah said. "You know, why don't Julian, Anne, Dick, and me go and get some tea and cookies and then we'll come back for a nice long chat."

Three of the Misfits' four mobile phones beeped and buzzed in quick succession with incoming texts. Hannah had put hers on silent when she'd arrived at the home. Brian took his phone from his pocket just as Sam and Amelia did. The message was from Chris. It read:

Get out of there. Now!

He knew by the expressions on the others' faces that they'd received the same message.

"No, you don't have to go to all that trouble. One of the

nurses will make the tea for us," Rodney said. "What else would they be doing with their time?"

Brian was on his feet before the others. "Nope, it'll only take us a minute. We really love making tea. Come on, guys, you can give me a hand."

As they edged toward the door, Rodney reached out, moving quicker than any of them suspected he was capable of moving. He tried to grab Amelia's arm, but her reflexes were good and she instinctively spun away, evading his grasp. Brian gave up on the pretense that they were making tea.

"Move, move," he hissed urgently.

"Get back here, you little freaks," Rodney roared.

He clambered to his feet as Brian ushered the girls and Sam through the door ahead of him. They walked down the hallway because they didn't want to run and raise suspicion. When they heard Rodney shout again, they increased their speed, getting faster and faster until they were swaying from side to side like some middle-aged people on a power walk.

"Everything okay?" the receptionist asked when they reached the lobby.

"Never better," Brian said.

"We're great," Amelia said.

"Just need a break," Hannah said.

"Rodney'll do that to you," the receptionist replied with a smile. "Are you leaving?"

"Yes," Sam said.

"No," Brian practically shouted.

Now he knew why Chris had sent them warning texts. The two gorillas that had chased him in their car—the two who'd moved the stolen goods from the cottage—were racing toward the nursing home's front door.

EIGHTEEN

Plunkett Healy had worked for Cornelius Figg, Ireland's richest man, for more than seven years and he'd hated almost every second of it. He'd thought of leaving his job on many occasions, usually after Mr. Figg had shouted at him or humiliated him in some way, yet he'd never actually quit. The trouble was that, even though Mr. Figg was a horrible boss, he paid very well and Healy liked being paid well. It meant he could buy lots of nice things, like clothes and gadgets and cars. But it also meant that if he wanted to continue to buy the nice things he had to do lots of unenjoyable tasks, like talking to criminals.

He picked up the phone and prepared to make the call. Someone called Lambert had started acquiring certain items for Mr. Figg a number of years earlier, items that were not strictly legal. If Cornelius Figg wanted something that wasn't legally up for sale—a memento from the *Titanic*, a piece of Viking jewelry uncovered by archaeologists—he'd tell Healy, and Healy would contact Lambert, who was always able to find and deliver whatever it was they were looking for. Healy never actually knew how Lambert managed to get the items. The fewer questions he asked, the better.

When they did business together, Plunkett Healy would put money in a briefcase and leave it at a prearranged point; Lambert would collect it and leave behind whatever memento it was that had been ordered. Healy would then deliver it to Mr. Figg, and his boss would place the memento in a secure room in his house along with all the others he'd accumulated over the years. Mr. Figg would visit the room once a month and stare at his collection for a few minutes. He was the only one allowed into the room and nobody else ever got to see the mementos. Plunkett Healy wasn't even sure his employer truly appreciated any of the items he purchased. He wasn't a very cultured man. He believed that Mr. Figg just liked the fact that he was the one who owned the objects that other rich men wanted.

The system had worked well over the years because most of the items were small and manageable. This time it was going to be a little different. This one could be dangerous, and that made Plunkett Healy nervous.

The phone number he dialed had changed from the last time he'd tried to contact Lambert over six months earlier. It was an Irish contact number this time. Previously, it had been an American one. That was about as much information as he had on Lambert, who was just a mysterious voice on the phone to him.

"Hello?" Lambert said.

"This is buyer number one-five-four-two," Plunkett Healy said.

"Go ahead."

There was no idle chitchat.

"Is the, um, delivery still on schedule for tomorrow night?"

"Yes."

"And it's in good condition?"

"Yes."

Plunkett Healy didn't know what to say next.

"Is there anything else?" Lambert asked.

"Did you bring it from Africa yourself?"

"I don't want to talk about that."

"No, okay. Thanks. See you tomorrow. Well, I won't see you, but . . ."

The line went dead. Before Healy had time to gather his thoughts, the door to his office burst open and Healy's second-least-favorite person in the world strode in. Barney Figg was Cornelius Figg's thirteen-year-old son. Mr. Figg considered Barney to be the smartest, sweetest boy in the world. Everyone else who met Barney considered him to be an idiot.

"Well, Healy, is it here yet?" Barney Figg demanded.

He was tanned from a vacation he'd been on in the Bahamas to recover from losing a soccer tournament earlier in the summer.

"No, sir, not yet. As I told you earlier, it'll be here tomorrow night."

"My party's going to be amazing, but it had better be here on time or it'll ruin everything. It's the centerpiece of the night. If not, the party will be a disaster and if the party's a disaster I'll blame you, Healy."

"Yes, I believe you will, young Mr. Figg."

As Barney exited the office, slamming the door shut after him, Plunkett Healy wondered, for what felt like the millionth time, if he shouldn't just get a normal job working normal hours for normal people.

NINETEEN

Lionel and Burt reached the front door of the nursing home. Burt, the heavier of the two, tried to wrench it open, then looked quite confused when that didn't work. Lionel, a slimmer man with longer hair, shook his head disparagingly and shoved his companion aside. He took the opposite approach and shoved the door, but that didn't work, either. By the time they'd figured out that you had to press the buzzer to get in, the four Misfits were off and running, no longer worried about raising suspicions.

They heard the receptionist call after them, but they ignored her. Running out of the lobby, they raced down another corridor, one that led away from the front door. They were looking for an exit, *any* exit. Amelia was the quickest, her legs a blur, her hands karate-chopping the air in a way that Brian would have mocked if they weren't being chased.

She took a sharp left, pushing through some swinging doors, the others just behind her. They found themselves in a huge kitchen. It was empty except for a janitor who was diligently mopping the floor. A door on the far side was being held open by a chair propped under its handle in order to let the air in to help dry it out more quickly. Beyond that was the outside world. They'd found an exit.

Without hesitating, they ran across the wet floor, slipping and sliding their way to freedom.

"Hey, no, I just spent the last hour cleaning that," the janitor cried.

"Sorry, really sorry," Amelia shouted as they left streaky footprints behind.

"We're all sorry," Brian yelled over his shoulder.

They raced around the side of the building, and toward the parking lot in the front. It took them a few seconds before they spotted Chris, the whistle between his lips, about to peep three times for the gravest danger. He'd been hiding behind a hedge and had only appeared when he'd heard his friends' voices.

"You made it," he said.

He was delighted. When he'd seen the two men rush into the nursing home, he'd assumed the worst.

"It won't be long before Rodney tells them what happened," Hannah said.

"We've got to get out of here," Amelia said.

"There's only one road in or out of this place," Brian said. "And that car they drive is quick. We'll never make it without being caught. We won't be fast enough."

"Over the hedge it is, then," Sam said. He began to climb the hedge, his hands and feet disappearing in the thick greenery. "I'll pull the rest of you up when I make it to the top . . . This is . . . harder than it looks."

He'd only made it about two feet up the hedge and had almost completely vanished, when Hannah grabbed him by the T-shirt and hauled him back down.

"Thanks for that. That thing's like green quicksand," Sam said.

"We have to hide. The parking lot's full enough. Move the bikes out of sight and duck behind the cars. With a bit of luck, they won't see us," Brian said.

They followed his lead, picking up their bikes, and wheeled them behind a row of cars in an area marked *Staff Parking*. Those were the vehicles that Brian figured were least likely to be moved in the next few moments. On the far side of the parking lot, sitting at an odd angle and badly parked, was the Subaru Impreza, the car with which Brian had already had one close encounter.

They got down on their haunches behind a black SUV. Five faces peeped out, focused on the entrance to the nursing home. One was a little more obvious than the others.

"Hannah," Amelia said. "Might be an idea to remove the jacket. You're not really camouflaged."

"Oh, right. Good idea," Hannah said, quickly removing her luminous reflective jacket. She stuffed it beside her bike. "Stupid safety clothing."

After a couple of minutes, there was still no movement at the entrance to the nursing home and the adrenaline rush was beginning to wear off for most of them. Sam was keeping an eye on the side door, but there was no sign of life there either.

"What's taking them so long?" Chris wondered aloud.

It wasn't that he wanted to see the men rush out, but the waiting was making him feel even more flustered and anxious.

"I've got an idea," Brian said.

"Another one? This must be some kind of record for you," Sam said.

"I know. I'm just as surprised as you are," Brian replied. "Once those guys drive away, we don't have any way of finding them again. And Rodney certainly isn't going to be giving us any information."

"He really was a horrible man," Amelia said.

"Was he?" Chris asked. "In what way?"

"Focus, Misfits," Hannah said. "Brian, keep talking."

"This is our best chance to find the stolen goods. If we follow the guys, then they might lead us to where we want to go."

"And how do we do that?" Amelia asked.

"I don't know. That's as far as I've gotten."

"Follow the bad guys? That's the entire plan?"

"It's a good plan," Brian replied, a little defensively. "We just need to iron out a few little details."

"Yes, like how a bunch of twelve-year-olds on bikes can follow a superpowered car," Hannah said.

"That would be one of the details. Probably the most important one, really."

"I've got it," Chris said. "There's an app on my tablet that can locate my phone. I installed it in case I ever lost my phone. See? You lot always think I'm too safety conscious, but when it comes to something like thi—"

"Gloat later, pal. We don't have much time to spare," Brian said.

"Right. Well, if we hide the phone in their car, then we can track their location on my tablet."

"Excellent. Give me your phone. I'll put it in the car," Brian said.

"I'll help you," Sam said. "No one's better at hiding stuff than me. I once hid a chocolate bar in a cupboard so that Chris wouldn't eat it. Didn't find it again for two years."

"Great, except we do want to find the phone again," Amelia said.

Chris was working furiously on his phone, his fingers almost a blur. He finished checking the setup, then unzipped his backpack and took out his tablet.

"Come on, come on," Chris said, urging his tablet to hurry up. "The app's almost loaded."

"We can put the phone in the car now, though, can't we?" Brian said.

"Oh, yeah. Of course. Go, go, go."

Chris held out the phone. Brian took it, or at least he tried to. Chris didn't let go. Normally, he wasn't too strong, but he had a super grip on his top-of-the-line Android phone.

"Chris?"

"It's a really, really nice phone. I know it was my idea, but I don't want to lose it."

"Oh, for goodness' sake," Hannah said. She thumped Chris on the shoulder.

"That hurt," he said, letting go immediately.

"Why didn't I think of that?" Sam said.

Brian took off, scurrying across the parking lot. He glanced at the entrance as he rushed past. Was that one of the men standing by the reception desk? He couldn't be sure. Sam was just behind him. They reached the car, Sam going to the passenger side, Brian to the driver's. They both tried the doors, but they were locked. They looked at each other over the roof.

"Trunk," Sam said.

The trunk opened with a gentle click. There was nothing in there other than a rolled-up blanket squashed into a corner. The spare tire was hidden under a dark gray floor mat. Brian lifted the mat up. He could squeeze the phone down by the side of the tire and cover it up again with the mat. The men wouldn't find it there unless they happened to get a flat and needed to change the tire.

"What's that?" Sam asked.

Brian hadn't heard it the first time, but he did the

second. It was the sound of someone attempting the world's worst birdcall.

"Chris," they both said at the same time.

Brian looked back to where the other Misfits were supposed to be hiding. They weren't hiding at all. Hannah, Chris, and Amelia were standing in between two parked cars, frantically waving their arms. They were warning them about something.

Brian heard a click as the lights at the back of the Impreza flashed twice. Sam must have known it was the men opening their car from a distance, Brian thought. Why else would his friend have suddenly shoved him into the trunk of the car?

Sam jumped in himself moments later. He pulled the trunk shut after him and plunged their world into darkness.

"Okay," Hannah said. "That wasn't part of the plan."

"What just happened?" Amelia asked. Her view had been obscured by Chris's head.

"Sam and Brian are now in the trunk of the car," Hannah said.

"Well, that's not good," Chris said.

The three of them watched as the men reached the car. They didn't check the trunk, so it didn't look as if they'd spotted Sam and Brian climbing in, although no one could be sure. Lionel jumped into the driver's seat;

Burt climbed in the passenger side. They didn't waste any time. The engine revved into life and the car reversed out of the parking space, before speeding toward the exit.

And then it was gone, with Brian and Sam still stuck in the trunk.

"No, that's not good at all," Chris said.

TWENTY

Chris checked his tablet. The app was installed and working.

"The tracking's on," he said.

"We'd better hurry up and follow them, then," Hannah said.

She'd put her reflective jacket and helmet back on and was in the middle of righting her bike. She hopped on and began to pedal. Chris and Amelia knew there was no point discussing their options. Hannah was right. There was only one plan now: follow that car.

Brian and Sam didn't speak for the next few minutes. They were concentrating all their energy on trying to stop themselves from being bounced around inside the trunk, partly to avoid injuring themselves, but mainly because they didn't want the men to hear them and figure out they had a couple of stowaways on board.

They tried, and failed, to make themselves comfortable. They bumped into the car's panels—and each other—as the Impreza hurtled down the road. It was only when one of the men switched on the stereo and turned a '90s song up to an earsplitting level that Brian and Sam decided it was safe enough to speak. The music boomed through the car and they could feel it reverberating deep in their bones.

"I know we're trapped and everything, but isn't this awesome? It's a real adventure. Much better than hanging around the den, talking all the time," Sam said.

"Awesome? *Awesome?* Are you insane? Why did you push me into the trunk?" Brian asked in an angry whisper.

"I had no other choice," Sam said.

"We could have run away in the opposite direction."

"Oh yeah, I suppose we could have. Still, we're here now. Better make the most of it. So what's the plan?"

"Plan? I didn't even know that I was going to be in the trunk of a car until thirty seconds ago. When do you think I came up with a plan?" Brian snapped.

"Take it easy, man. Getting angry is not going to solve this problem we've gotten ourselves into."

"Not *we*, Sam, *you*. *You've* gotten us into this."

The car swerved around a bend, taking it too quickly and sending Sam and Brian slamming into each other.

"You okay?" Brian asked when they'd managed to untangle themselves.

"Yeah, luckily my head bounced off some kind of rug or blanket. Cushioned the impact."

Another terrible '90s song boomed through the car. The men really did have the worst taste in music.

"They're definitely the guys you saw before, aren't they?" Sam asked.

"Yes, they're the same guys," Brian said, exasperated. "Right. Not getting caught should be our number-one priority. When the car stops, we'll be ready in case they open the trunk. If that happens, we come out fighting."

"Got it," Sam said.

The music was switched off suddenly. The next sound they heard was one of the men speaking. His voice was muffled, but it was loud enough for them to make out most of what he was saying.

"What did you turn it off for, Lionel? I love East 17," the heavier of the two said.

"Shut up, Burt—I heard something," Lionel said.

"You're always hearing things. Remember when you thought you heard that guy when we broke into that house and it turned out there was no one there? Or when you said you'd heard a phone ringing when we were in the cottage in the forest?"

"It sounded like voices."

"Yeah, like there's people in the car with us. This isn't a horror movie, Lionel. I'm not going to turn around and find someone hiding in the backseat . . . Aaaarrrrgggggghhhh . . . There he is. He's been hiding there all the time. We're gonna die."

"You're not funny. You do know that, right?"

"I'm hilarious. You just don't have a sense of humor—that's your problem."

The car swung right, but Sam and Brian were prepared this time. They pressed their hands and feet against the interior panels, bracing themselves as much as they could.

"I'm starving," Burt said. "Super Burger or Chicken Express?"

"We can't eat now. We have to check the house. We'll probably have to move the stuff again now that those kids are onto us. How do you think they found us?"

"Who cares? They're just some dumb kids. Rodney was probably overreacting. You know what he's like. Come on, let's stop for a quick bite. I haven't eaten in over an hour."

"Those kids are like the Scooby-Doo gang or something," Lionel said. "If they get the cops involved—"

"They don't know where we've moved the stuff to. It's safe. And I don't want to move it all again. It's a giant pain."

"You really are a lazy whiner."

"Lazy? Of course I'm lazy. I didn't start thieving because I wanted to work hard, you know. I took to crime to make my life easier, but now it's manual labor this, manual labor that," Burt grumbled.

The next part of the conversation was drowned out by the blare of the radio. The driver had switched it on again. Brian guessed Lionel had turned it on so he wouldn't have to listen to Burt any longer.

"Looks like we could be here for a while," Sam whispered.

"Looks like it," Brian agreed.

As the minutes ticked by, Brian's arms and legs grew tired from being stuck in the same position. He was starting to cramp up. He badly wanted to get out of there. He hoped the others were tracking them.

"I'm not good on hills," Chris wheezed.

The girls had stopped their bikes at the crest of a hill one hundred yards ahead while they waited for him to catch up. At first glance, the road didn't look challenging, but it was a long, gradual incline that had sapped Chris's energy quite quickly. He wasn't used to cycling—Sam was the sporty one in the family—and it showed. Sweat needled his brow and his legs had begun to cramp.

Cars whizzed by, providing brief, cooling gusts of air and lungfuls of exhaust fumes as he finally caught up with Amelia and Hannah.

"I've been weighed down by loads of safety stuff and Amelia's bike is from the seventeen hundreds or something. You shouldn't be that far behind us," Hannah said.

"I know," Chris said. "It's really embarrassing. That red on my face is shame mixed with overexertion, which possibly indicates I need some medical attention. Anyone else seeing stars?"

"Miss Marple never had to put up with this," Hannah muttered to herself.

Chris wiped the sweat from his brow, then took the tablet from his backpack. Amelia and Hannah looked over his shoulder as they followed the onscreen progress of the little green dot that represented Chris's mobile phone. It had moved on from the gridlines of the town to the surrounding countryside.

"That's at least two more miles of cycling," Chris groaned.

"Shouldn't you be more worried about your brother?" Amelia asked.

"What? Oh yeah. Wow, that was selfish of me. No, Sam and Brian are fine. As long as the little green dot is moving then they won't have been discovered. They're only in trouble when it stops moving."

The onscreen dot stopped moving just as Chris finished the sentence.

"Well, that's just bad timing," he said dolefully.

He stared at the tablet for a moment before shaking the screen, as if that would make it move. It was an instinctive reaction and, he knew, a futile one.

"Does that mean—"

"Yep," Chris said.

He was twenty yards ahead, racing down the hill before either of the girls had climbed back on their bikes.

Even though the car had come to a stop, and they knew that they had to prepare themselves for the moment the trunk was opened, Brian and Sam found it difficult to get into position. Their muscles were trembling and weren't totally obeying the orders their brains were sending. They moved around shakily in the cramped conditions.

Brian heard the car doors slam shut, followed by the sound of footsteps. The men were heading toward the back of the car. Suddenly, Sam's face loomed out of the darkness. Brian suppressed a yelp. His friend had found Chris's mobile phone. He must have pressed a button rather than engaged the flashlight setting as the light that illuminated his features was weak.

"Ready?" Sam whispered, one hand balled up into a twitching fist.

Brian nodded yes, which was a lie. He didn't feel ready at all. But they had to act. The men were bigger and stronger, but they weren't expecting to find them in there either, so Brian and Sam had the element of surprise on their side. The moment they opened the trunk, they'd launch themselves forward, shouting like Celtic warriors, and hope to create enough confusion to escape with a head start.

But the trunk didn't open and the footsteps faded. The men had gone somewhere else. As soon as he thought the coast was clear Sam reached forward, about to open the trunk.

"Wait," Brian said, grabbing his friend's arm. "What if we're somewhere that's out in the open? They might see us the second we get out of the car."

"You're right. We should just stay in here until they discover us," Sam said sarcastically.

"Fair point."

It was too risky to wait for something to happen. They had to take action. Brian released his friend's arm, but when Sam tried to open the trunk, he had no luck.

"It's stuck," he said.

Together they pushed at the trunk lid, even resorting to lying on their backs, their knees pressed into their chest and the soles of their feet against the lid, but it wouldn't budge.

"What now?" Sam gasped. He was puffed out from the effort.

"I've got an idea," Brian said.

Chris was lagging behind the girls again, but not as far behind as he had been earlier. They were coasting along narrow, potholed country roads, allowing him to catch up a little. It was a pleasant summer's evening, and if it hadn't been for two of their friends being accidentally kidnapped, the girls would have been enjoying their ride in the countryside.

"Left turn," Chris called out from behind.

The girls just about heard him in time to make it. The road they turned onto was hemmed in on either side by overgrown hedges that would have scratched at their faces if they hadn't ducked beneath them.

Amelia and Hannah slowed until he'd caught up with them.

"Thanks. I've no idea why some people exercise for pleasure. This is absolute torture," he said. "You ever been here before?"

"Not that I remember," Hannah said.

He looked down the long, narrow road ahead. It seemed to disappear right into the heart of the countryside.

"What do you think is down there?" he asked.

"Doesn't matter," Amelia said. "We have to help the boys. They're not smart enough to get out of trouble by themselves."

Hannah started to disagree, but then gave up. She was only doing it out of a sense of loyalty. Those two were always doing something stupid. Usually, though, the stupid thing was fairly minor. This looked major.

Brian's plan was actually working. He could hardly believe it himself. Since they couldn't open the trunk, they'd looked for an alternative route out of their temporary prison. He'd guessed correctly that the backseats would fold down and after much maneuvering, involving a pulled muscle, trapped fingers, and some choice swearwords, they'd managed to force their way into the back of the car. They pushed the seats back into place before peeping through the tinted windows.

The car was parked in a farmyard, although it didn't look

as if any farming had taken place there in the last few years. There was an old milking shed to one side, its gray galvanized roof speckled with yellow and brown patches of rust. An empty haybarn was on the opposite side. Discarded farm equipment littered the yard and the old two-story house looked tired and baggy and in need of renovation.

"What are they doing in there?" Brian said.

"Let's figure that out later. Time for us to move," Sam said. He changed his mind when he saw the men coming out of the house. The heavier one had a grimace on his face and blood was dripping from his hand. "Okay, back in the trunk, back in the trunk."

They'd barely made it back in before the car doors opened and Lionel and Burt climbed in again.

Luckily for the other Misfits, they knew the Impreza was coming down the road toward them long before they saw or even heard it. Chris had been checking the tracking app again when he'd seen the little green dot begin moving in their direction.

"Hide! They're coming back," he said.

Amelia recognized the distinctive throaty roar of the engine in the distance moments later. The trio managed to bundle themselves, bikes and all, into the ditch just before the car raced past. If either of the men had seen them, they gave no sign, the car barely slowing down before it turned left sharply and slalomed out of sight.

Hannah righted her bike, her hands covered in thorn scratches. "Did we just bike all the way here, only for them to drive off somewhere else immediately?"

"Looks like it," Amelia said.

"We have to follow them. If Sam and Brian are still in that car, the—" Chris began.

"He's right," Amelia said.

With heavy hearts, they turned their bikes around. Chris checked the movement of his phone on the tablet again. The green dot on the screen was speeding back toward Newpark. They'd have to cycle back the way they'd come.

TWENTY-ONE

After a while, Brian and Sam got used to bouncing off each other in the trunk of the car and were growing bored. If it wasn't for their hunger and desperate need to pee, they'd have almost been comfortable.

They'd come to a stop and the men had gotten out of the car again and Brian and Sam hadn't heard them for almost five minutes. They decided to wait for just long enough to make sure the men were actually gone, but not so long that they'd return and catch them escaping from the car. It was difficult to know exactly how to calculate that, so they didn't. Instead, they relied on Sam's not-very-reliable gut instinct.

"Let's get out of here," Sam said after another minute, echoing exactly what Brian had been thinking.

Using their by-now-familiar escape route, they climbed into the backseat of the car and had a quick look around. They were in a vast housing development, and it looked familiar.

"Is this—"

"Yes," Brian said.

They both knew where they were—Castle Park—the largest estate in Newpark. Hundreds of semidetached houses were spread on either side of a network of speed-bumped roads and green areas. Neither of them had any idea what Lionel and Burt were doing here, but Brian noticed that the car was parked on a sidewalk rather than in a driveway. Whether that meant anything or not, he wasn't sure.

They opened the back door, keeping an eye out for the men. The curtains were drawn in the nearest house. They couldn't see any sign of life inside, but there was plenty of life on the street. Nobody gave Brian and Sam a second look as they emerged from the car.

Brian's legs were weak and tingled with pins and needles. It was good to be free, but there was no time to hang around and celebrate. They had to get out of there as quickly as they could.

He was almost at the end of the road when he looked back and saw that Sam was leaning into the passenger side of the car, his head hidden by the open door. What was he doing?

His friend emerged moments later with Chris's mobile phone in his hand. Brian gestured at him frantically until Sam looked up. He grinned and waved back before ducking his head back in the car again.

"Come on, Sam. What's taking you so long?" Brian muttered to himself.

He was still feeling sick from being trapped in the trunk for so long and now he was getting edgy, too. He knew they'd been lucky to escape without being captured. It'd be foolish to get caught n—

The front door of the house opened and there was one of the men, the heavier of the two. It was okay—he hadn't seen Sam. He was just lighting up a cigarette. If Brian could distract him in some way, then Sam might get away. No, too late. He'd spotted him. Nice one, Sam.

"I know you," Burt said. "How do I know you?" His brow furrowed while it waited for his brain to catch up. "Hey. You're one of the nursing-home kids." He roared for his brother. "*Get out here. Now.*"

It took Sam a moment to react. It was a moment he didn't have to spare.

Lionel was quicker than Burt. He was out the door and past him in a heartbeat.

"Run," Brian shouted.

His friend didn't need to be told twice. He rushed forward, his feet slapping the sidewalk, heading in Brian's direction. Brian turned and took off. Sam was alongside him within seconds. They reached the end of the road. Left or right?

Lionel was in hot pursuit, Burt lumbering after him.

Sam ducked left, Brian following his lead. They both glanced over their shoulders to see if Lionel was gaining on them. They shouldn't have looked.

For a moment, Brian thought he'd run into a concrete wall. Then he realized it was a concrete wall in human form.

"Well, well, well, isn't this my lucky day," Declan "Smasher" Grabbe said as Brian and Sam bounced off him and crumpled to the ground, sore and winded.

When Lionel and Burt turned the corner, it was to find a mountain of a boy with a secure grip on the two youngsters they'd been pursuing.

Burt grinned nastily, revealing that he still had almost two-thirds of his own teeth.

"Thanks for the help, pal," Lionel said. "We'll take it from here."

"Take what from here?" Smasher said.

"We want a word with those two kids."

"You can have a word with them when I'm finished, though they won't be in a talking mood then," Smasher said.

"Listen to me, mate," Lionel began, but Burt had already lunged forward.

Smasher released his grip on Sam and Brian, and took out Burt with a right hook. Burt fell back against his brother, who, rather than catching him, shoved him aside.

"That was mistake number one," Lionel said. "You don't get to make two of them."

"I think we should run," Sam whispered.

"I think you're right," Brian agreed.

They took off and were already twenty yards away when Lionel was felled by another Smasher punch. They were safe for the moment. Smasher was big and strong, but he wasn't fast. There was no way he was catching them. He didn't even try.

"What were you doing?" Brian asked a few minutes later when they were clear of danger.

"What do you mean?"

The back of Sam's T-shirt was covered in clumps of what looked like black-and-white fur. Brian picked some off and showed it to him.

"This stuff is all over your shirt."

Sam examined it. "Oh, I know. Must be from that blanket that was in the trunk. Those guys—"

"Manuel and Bart, it sounded like."

They had misheard the men's names due to the poor acoustics in the car.

"Yeah, they must have a dog or something. Looks like the color of one of those Labradors or Newfoundlands or something. Chris'd know. Anyway, that's hardly important now, is it?"

He must have cared a little bit, though, because he whipped off his T-shirt, turned it inside out, and put it back on again.

"That wasn't the best idea. It's scratchy now," he said.

"We should call the others," Brian said.

"Knowing them, they're probably sitting around the nursing home having cups of tea and cookies while we're out doing all the running around," Sam said.

Hannah was thrilled when they called. She kept saying,

"You're okay, you're okay," in a relieved voice, which unnerved the boys a little as she wasn't normally one for being emotional. Insults they could deal with, but a caring nature—well, that was something else entirely. It was awkward. They arranged to meet up back at the nursing home where Brian and Sam could retrieve their bikes.

Chris and the two girls wanted to hear about everything the boys had gotten up to and they peppered them with questions as they rode home. They were extremely interested in where the men had been driving to. They'd also be checking the Internet for any characters called Manuel and Bart in the next few hours.

"They're distinctive names. We should easily find something on them," Chris said.

"We've stumbled onto something serious," Hannah said. "Did you see how quickly Manuel and Bart turned up at the nursing home once Rodney went into the hallway? You don't have two guys chasing after you unless they think you're going to stop them from doing something."

"We know Rodney was involved and we have some of the places they visited tracked on the tablet, but where do we go from here?" Amelia asked.

"We go back to my place and get something to eat," Hannah said. "Anyone hungry?"

"I'm ravenous," Brian said.

"Me too," Sam said. "And I really, really need to find a bathroom."

"Mom'll have my dinner ready by now. It must be nearly half past five. I'd better hurry if I don't want to be late," Hannah said.

She almost fainted when she looked at her phone. She'd completely lost track of the time. It was 6:03 p.m. and there were three missed calls from her mother and two from her father.

"I'm dead," Hannah said. "So, so, so, so dead. Name something dead, double how dead it is, and that's me. I've got to go. Don't send any texts or app messages about what we've been up to just in case they take my phone away as punishment. If I can't get to my phone, keep an eye out for e-mails, letters, and messages in bottles. I'll get in touch somehow."

She took off immediately and within a minute she was just a luminous yellow dot in the distance, her jacket and helmet picked out by the fading sun.

"What do we do now?" Amelia said.

"We go home. I'll examine all the data on the tablet," Chris said. "Sam will write out a full and detailed report of everything he can remember—"

"Great, who doesn't love writing essays during the summer vacation," Sam said.

"—and we'll meet up early tomorrow morning and decide on our next move."

"An early morning as well? Right after Mom and Dad's farewell party? This just gets better and better."

AMELIA'S JOURNAL

I actually love it here. I never thought I'd say that.
I can hardly believe I wrote it. Every day is fun now. I
always thought Newpark was really boring, but I guess
I was just hanging out with the wrong people.

   I spoke to my dad on the phone and we got along a
bit better. Things are looking up. He's even started
hinting about coming home, but the thing is I don't
really want to go home. Not now when things are just
getting interesting. I'm getting along great with
Gran. I still hate her food (if it wasn't for Hannah's
mom, I think I'd have probably starved to death by
now) and sometimes Gran can be hard to deal with
because she thinks she's right about everything. The
worst thing is that she usually IS right about stuff.
That's <u>very</u> annoying. She still thinks I'm a bit uptight
and scared to take chances. She's always saying
things like, "You've got to loosen up, Amelia," or, "Do
the things you fear and the death of fear is certain,"
which I think means something like do scary things
and you won't find them as scary anymore. Well, I
<u>have</u> been doing scary things and I intend to do plenty
more. It's so weird. I think if my friends saw me now
they wouldn't recognize me. I don't look very different and maybe from the outside I might not seem

that different, but I feel different. I feel like I can do anything. I don't know why that is.

The only thing that's really bothering me is the secret I've been keeping about why I'm here. I've come close to telling Hannah a couple of times, but I've lost my nerve (which sounds like a joke after writing about how much better I am at doing scary things). What if I tell her and she hates me? What if they all hate me and never want to talk to me again? Gran says that secrets are bad for the soul. I think she might be right. Why is she always right?

TWENTY-TWO

Brian arrived home to a sound he'd never heard before or ever expected to hear—the sound of Mucky McDonnell vacuuming. He wasn't vacuuming particularly well, since he was standing still and just moving the vacuum cleaner backward and forward over the same spots again and again, but it was still a revelation to Brian. He stared at his father openmouthed until Mucky noticed he was there and switched the machine off.

"Don't say a word," Mucky said.

Brian went up to his room and lay down on his bed.

After being stuck in the trunk of a car, it was almost heavenly to be on his comfortable bed. His joy was short-lived, though, as soon after, he had to get up and take a shower and get dressed for the party, which he'd almost forgotten about. He did his best not to laugh when he went downstairs and saw Mucky dressed in his only suit, his remaining hair tied back in a ponytail. The suit was as old as Brian, and Mucky had been a bit lighter back then, so now it strained at the seams. The material would probably burst if Mucky made any sudden movement.

"Sharon's meeting us there," Mucky said. He twirled around. "What do you think, kid? Am I good enough for the pages of GQ magazine?"

"Suppose so," Brian said. He had more on his mind than his father's fashion choices.

"Grumpy little twerp," Mucky muttered.

The party was already underway when Brian and Mucky arrived and the Adamus' house was teeming with people. Children ran in and out of the large white tent that took up nearly every square inch of the backyard. Tables were laden down with a huge variety of food—roasted chickens, salads, baked sweet potatoes, suya, quiches, burgers—and a vast array of drinks from apple juice to zobo. Mr. Adamu loved cooking food from his hometown in Nigeria—and it all smelled delicious.

"Patrick, great to see you," Mrs. Adamu said, a smile lighting up her face as they reached the back door. She'd been in elementary school with Mucky and was one of the few people in Newpark who ever seemed pleased to see him.

It took a moment for Brian to realize she was talking to his father. He was so used to people calling him Mucky that he hardly remembered his real name was Patrick.

Mrs. Adamu gave Mucky a big hug and kiss, and winked at Brian.

"Plenty of food and drink for everyone. This is a party, so don't be shy. Brian, show your father around."

She moved along to greet someone else as they squeezed

into the house. Two of Sam and Chris's brothers were scurrying around carrying plates piled high with food and delivering them to the adults before returning to get more. Adeyinka, their eleven-year-old sister, smiled hello at Brian as she passed by. Lively music blared from speakers balanced precariously on the back of a couch. A couple of people were attempting to dance. Their attempts were not good.

"Brian, over here," Amelia called out from a corner of the living room.

"I'll see if Sharon's here yet," Mucky said.

Brian joined Amelia. It took an effort to make his way through the throngs of people, all having a good time. Amelia looked more glamorous than usual. Her red hair was styled and she was wearing a dress. An expensive-looking bag was draped over her shoulder.

"Some party," Brian said.

"Sure is. Sam and Chris are helping out in the tent. Hannah's lining up for the bathroom."

They didn't say anything for a moment, both of them suddenly a little shy. They weren't used to being in each other's company without any other Misfits around.

"How much longer do you have to look after your grandmother for?" Brian asked.

He immediately regretted the question. It was the kind of boring one an adult might have asked.

"Oh, a couple more weeks, I'd say. She's not as strong as people think," Amelia replied.

"Hello, everyone," Florence boomed as she made a grand entrance.

She grabbed a glass of wine from a passing tray and began talking quite loudly to the first person who happened to cross her path.

"Yes, she does look kind of frail," Brian said.

Amelia stared at the glass of soda in her hand. Brian was glad when Hannah returned from the bathroom a minute later and the awkwardness faded.

"You must not be in that much trouble with your parents if you're at the party," Brian said.

"That's where you're wrong," Hannah said. "They haven't said anything yet, but I know the game they're playing. I'll be punished tomorrow. Just you wait and see. They're tricky like that."

Over the next few hours food was eaten, speeches were made, songs were sung, and tears were shed as people celebrated the Adamus having been an important part of the community. And then crowds began to thin out as people drifted away home. Chris was relieved when his cousin-in-law, Officer Debra O'Loughlin, left the party. He'd suspected she'd been keeping an eye on them during the evening, but she had to leave before some of the others as she had an early start the next morning.

Amelia, Hannah, and Brian—with a large slice of cake in his hand—made their way to the tent, where Sam and Chris were finishing up their serving duties.

"How come you had to work at your own party?" Amelia asked.

Chris wiped the sweat from his brow. "Our mom has a big thing about being a good host and we didn't want to let her down."

"Also, if we didn't work, she'd kill us," Sam said.

"Oh no," Hannah whispered. "Look at them."

The parents of the Misfits had formed their own little gang at the back of the tent. Hannah's father was snapping pictures of everyone on his mobile phone. There was lots of cackling and plenty of laughter. Mucky was in the middle of it all, telling a story everyone seemed to find amusing. Sharon was beside him, still wearing her coat, even though the evening wasn't particularly cold.

"I can't respect a man who was attacked by a goose," Florence chuckled.

"It wasn't a goose—it was a duck," Mucky said.

"The type of bird isn't really the issue," Florence replied.

This was followed by more laughter. Hannah couldn't understand it. Her parents appeared to be having a good time.

"Why do parents have to be so embarrassing?" Sam asked.

"I think it's the law," Brian said. "They probably take a course in how to embarrass their children."

"There they are," Mr. Adamu shouted across when he noticed the Misfits.

"Our intrepid investigators," Mrs. Fitzgerald whooped.

"What's wrong with her? She's smiling and laughing. That's not the way she normally behaves," Hannah said. "Don't worry, she doesn't know anything about the real investigation."

"Still don't like them talking about it," Brian said.

Whether he liked it or not, they continued to talk about it for the next few minutes, and the others were soon as annoyed as Brian. No amount of *please desist* gestures or glaring eye contact could stop their parents.

"Remember when they went investigating because they thought there was a secret agent in town?" Mr. Fitzgerald said.

"That's right. The Amazing Mystery of the Eye Spy," Mr. Adamu chortled.

Sharon looked over at Brian. She smiled when he caught her eye. *That's weird*, he thought. *Why is she being nice?* Was she actually feeling sorry for him?

"Or when the cat burglar they were chasing for two weeks turned out to be an actual cat," Mrs. Adamu said.

Mr. Fitzgerald slapped his thigh and whooped with laughter. The Misfits Club was not impressed. Hannah was as stony-faced as a gargoyle.

"They think we're a joke," Chris said.

Sam was lost for words for the first time in over a year. He couldn't believe they were mocking the club.

The parents were still talking, but now Mrs. Fitzgerald

had turned her attention to Mucky. Brian's blood froze. He knew what was coming next.

"Which of their mysteries was your favorite, Patrick?" Mrs. Fitzgerald asked.

Mucky looked confused and a little embarrassed. He didn't have an answer. He'd barely remembered that Brian was in some kind of club. His mouth opened and closed, but no sound escaped. He stood there looking increasingly uncomfortable as the seconds ticked by and the other parents waited for him to say something, until Florence came to his rescue.

"The biggest mystery of them all is how Patrick 'Mucky' McDonnell ever got to be so handsome," she said. "I remember him wandering around the town as a young fella and he was really funny-looking back then."

She elbowed him to emphasize her point and Mucky went flying, almost crashing through the side of the tent. All the parents loved that and they cracked up laughing. By the time Mucky had righted himself, Florence had skillfully changed the subject.

Hannah's father was getting people to pose for a photo whether they wanted to or not, still snapping away with his mobile phone. He took one of Florence and Mrs. F, then the Adamus. Mucky didn't need to be persuaded—he was happy to pose. Sharon pulled her coat collar in tighter, as if she was trying to keep out the cold, and Mucky squeezed her shoulder with one hand and made the bunny-ears sign behind her head with the other.

While the others were annoyed at what they saw as their parents' mocking, Brian was just relieved that his father was joining in and hadn't made a fool of himself. It was Amelia who lifted the gloom that had descended.

"I think it's a good thing that they don't take us seriously," she said. "It'll make it a lot sweeter when we prove them wrong by solving this mystery."

"You're right. We'll show them we're not a joke," Sam said. "We'll do whatever it takes. We'll face every danger. What's the worst that could happen?"

"We could die horribly," Chris said.

"Really? Okay, that's pretty bad," Sam said.

The twins got called on to do some more tidying up and persuaded the others to give them a hand. Despite her eagerness to help, Amelia managed to break two plates and tip a half-eaten piece of chocolate-and-cream cake onto the back of a neighbor's brand-new shirt before Chris decided to intervene.

"Er, you've worked hard enough, Amelia. Why don't you take a break?" he said. "We've got it from here."

"Are you sure? Because I don't mind wash—"

"Very sure. Very, very sure. Sit down, relax, eat some eclairs," he said, ushering her away from the kitchen to a place where she was less likely to cause damage.

Amelia made herself comfortable on the couch. When

Brian glanced across at her a couple of minutes later, she had a strange expression on her face. She noticed him looking and smiled, but it didn't look like a normal smile, at least not to him.

Something's bothering her, he thought, but he swiftly forgot about it.

The party was almost at an end when Amelia left the couch and went to the bathroom to wash her hands. To her surprise, there was still a line for the bathroom. When she emerged shortly after, Brian was next in line. She smiled, but once again it was a strange kind of smile, before she stumbled over a rampaging five-year-old. She almost hit the ground, but Brian caught her in time. Her shoulder bag slid down her arm. It was open, but she managed to stop it from sliding off completely and all of its contents from emptying onto the ground.

For a moment, Brian was stunned. Surely that wasn't . . . ? Amelia clipped the bag shut and carried on downstairs.

"Hey, do you need to use the bathroom or not?"

The person behind him in the line was practically hopping from one foot to the other.

"No, go ahead," Brian said.

"Thanks, pal. I couldn't have held on for much longer."

Brian leaned up against the wall. Had he really seen what he thought he'd seen in Amelia's bag? No, he'd made a mistake. That was it. He was tired and had a lot on his mind. It was a mistake.

TWENTY-THREE

At ten o'clock the next morning, Hannah sat on a couch in her old playroom, her arms folded, a stern expression on her face. Her mother strode into the room, gave the coffee table a wipe, and pulled the curtains open with a flourish.

"Why are you sitting there doing nothing?" she asked.

Hannah didn't reply.

"There's no point sulking, Hannah. You know the rules and the rules are there for your safety. If you're late, you're grounded. Your father and I were terrified that something had happened to you."

"I was only a few minutes late."

"You were forty-nine minutes late, and you failed to answer five telephone calls," Mrs. Fitzgerald said.

"Other people get to be late all the time and they never get grounded."

"Well, good for them."

She began to hum a Vietnamese song as she tidied up around Hannah, who remained pouting on the couch. When Mrs. Fitzgerald swung the window open, Hannah almost leaped from her seat with fright, but she managed to compose herself just in time.

"What a lovely day," Mrs. Fitzgerald said.

It *was* a lovely day. The sun was lazily arcing through the bluest sky there had been in weeks. Mrs. Fitzgerald held her cleaning cloth out of the window and shook it free of dust. If she hadn't started singing again, she might have heard the stifled cough that came from just below the sill.

"You have until three o'clock to complete your list of chores, then we're going to visit Mrs. Finnegan," was the last thing Hannah's mother said before she left the room.

As soon as the door was shut, Hannah raced to the window. Her friends were gathered in a pile on the path below. Amelia and Brian were holding Sam down while Chris had his hand clamped over his brother's mouth.

"We're clear," Hannah said.

They released Sam, who immediately began to cough into his T-shirt, trying his best to keep the noise to a minimum. He'd happened to be in the wrong spot when Mrs. Fitzgerald had shaken the cloth clean and, inhaling nearly all of the dust, he'd only been able to keep quiet thanks to the Misfits' intervention.

"Got any food, Hannah? I didn't have breakfast," Brian asked.

Hannah raided the emergency cupboard and handed him a couple of bags of chips. "Mom could swing by again at any moment, so if she comes in I'll start singing. That'll be your cue to shut up immediately," she said.

"Got it," Sam said.

"So I call this extraordinary meeting of the Misfits Club to order," Hannah said. "I've found nothing on Manuel and Bart so far. All I keep getting is stuff on characters from *The Simpsons* and a guy from some old show called *Fawlty Towers*. I'll keep at it. Not much else I can do when I'm trapped here anyway."

"When's the grounding over?" Brian asked.

"Two days in total, starting at nine this morning, so forty-six and a half hours from now," Hannah said.

"You're stuck here for two days? That's harsh."

Hannah checked over her shoulder. She'd thought she'd heard the faint click of the door handle turning, but it remained in place.

"Everything okay?" Amelia asked.

"Yeah. I keep thinking that Mom's going to catch me doing something she disapproves of and I'm going to end up with an extended sentence. It's making me jittery. Just make sure she doesn't spot you guys or I don't know when I'll get out of here again. The other thing is, remember I told you I found this place online where they analyze old paintings and stuff? I sent a copy of Amelia's drawing of the painting and I'm waiting to hear back. The only thing is you have to pay for it, so I had to do it on my dad's laptop and now I'm banned from using it, so I don't know if they've replied or not."

"There's no other way you can get in touch?"

"No, they give you an access code and—"

"The access code's on your dad's laptop," Amelia said.

"I'll see if I can sneak it out later, but it won't be easy. They're watching me like hawks."

They spent the next few minutes whispering about Rodney O'Reilly and what connection he could have had to the two men in the Impreza, but they knew everything they said was just guesswork at this point. They needed more information before they could figure out what was going on. Who were Manuel and Bart? Why were the stolen items such a random assortment of things? Why had they been hiding them in such an unusual location? And where were they now?

"We have to go back and check out the places they went yesterday, that old farm and the house they parked outside. They must have stopped there for a reason. Maybe that's where they're storing the stuff they stole," Sam said.

"We'll go to both places we stopped at and check them out," Brian said. "Chris, can you print off the address of the farm from the information you got on the tablet?"

"No problem."

"I'll go with you, if you don't mind," Amelia said.

"The more, the merrier," Sam said, patting her on the back.

Brian was confused. Amelia and Hannah had become really close over the last week and seemed to almost be joined at the hip, yet she wanted to spend her afternoon riding around with Sam and him, rather than stay with Hannah. Something didn't add up.

"Look, there's something else we need to talk about, too," Hannah began. "Something Amelia's discov—"

Hannah interrupted herself and broke into song. It took Brian a moment to realize that this meant something was wrong—Hannah wasn't breaking into song because of her happy-go-lucky nature. He felt a hand grasp his and, before he could protest, Amelia was pulling him along the footpath and around the back of the garden shed, where Sam and Chris were already hiding. When he looked back toward the window, he saw Mrs. Fitzgerald leaning out, a suspicious look creasing her features. Luckily, she didn't spot them.

The moment he was back home, Chris got stuck into his work: good old-fashioned research. He loved this more than anything. He couldn't really understand why Brian and Sam preferred all that running around.

The first house that Brian, Amelia, and Sam went to was the one in Castle Park, the housing development where Brian and Sam had escaped from the car the day before. There was no sign of the men's car, and the curtains were still drawn. The gate that led to the back of the house was padlocked.

Amelia spoke to a neighbor who was just returning home laden down with shopping bags. She told her she was looking for a friend from school and was wondering if she'd come to the right house. The neighbor was friendly and said that the woman who lived there had only moved in six months ago, and she'd never seen her with anyone else. She presumed she didn't have children, so Amelia's friend must be living elsewhere.

"She didn't mention anything about two men," Amelia said when the neighbor had gone back into her house. "So maybe Manuel and Bart don't live there."

"We should go around the back. See if there's anything suspicious there."

"Not now," Amelia said. "The woman is still watching us."

She was peeping out from behind her curtains; only one eye and part of her forehead was visible.

"We'll come back later," Brian decided.

It took them nearly an hour to get to the farmhouse. As soon as they arrived, they realized they'd wasted their time. They circled the house, looking for ways to get in. The front door, which was made of thick, solid wood, with a small, diamond-shaped piece of glass in its center, was securely locked. The windows were double-glazed and the back door was as securely fastened as the front door. All the curtains in the house were drawn tightly, without even a whisper of a gap. They couldn't see anything through the glass in the front door other than some scraps of paper and broken-down furniture.

"Should we smash the windows?" Sam asked eagerly.

"They won't be easy to smash through."

"I'm willing to give it a try."

Amelia ran her finger along one of the window frames, easily wiping a clean line through some of the dirt. She examined her finger, then examined the frame.

"It's clean underneath."

"So?"

"How would you describe the house?"

"Farmy?"

"Everything is overgrown and dirty and dusty. Like it hasn't been cleaned for years. That makes sense because the house looks like it hasn't been lived in for a while, but the windows look new and the dirt, well, it looks like someone put it there."

"Who'd be stupid enough to do that?" Sam asked. "Who deliberately puts dirt on a window?"

"People who have something to hide," Amelia said.

By the time they'd gotten halfway back to town, they were tired, hungry, and worn out. They stopped for a break, laying their bicycles against a tree and sprawling out themselves on a patch of grass. They only had one option left.

"He won't do it," Sam said. "He'll be too scared or

he'll think it's wrong or that we should call the cops or something."

"But he's the only one of us who knows anything about picking locks," Brian said.

They had tried to pick one of the locks themselves, using a safety pin that Amelia was carrying in her backpack, but after fifteen minutes of scratching around they had to admit defeat and give up.

"I'm telling you—he won't do it."

"I'll persuade him," Brian said. "Look, there's obviously something in that house that they're hiding. And you heard those guys yesterday when we were in the trunk of the car—they know we're after them, so they're not going to take any chances. They'll move the stuff and then they'll never be seen again and all this will be over."

"Fine, try to persuade him, then. See how well that works."

Brian borrowed Amelia's phone and gave his friend a call.

Chris said no.

"What's wrong with him? Why is he so uptight?" Brian asked when he'd hung up. They were on the verge of solving the case—he could feel it in his bones—and Chris was going to mess things up for them because he thought that breaking into a house that didn't belong to him was a very bad thing.

"Look, we'll go back home, get something to eat, and then I'll talk to him," Amelia said. "Face to face."

"And if you don't persuade him?" Brian asked.

"Then we'll figure out another way to get into those houses," Amelia said.

"Wow. You've changed," Sam said. "Like, in a good way."

Brian arrived home, still simmering with fury at Chris. As he shut the front door, he noticed an envelope bearing his name lying on the hall mat.

He noticed that it didn't have a stamp, so it hadn't been mailed, even though it had his full name and address written on the outside. The name *Brian* had been misspelled as *Bryan*. He didn't want to bump into his dad or Sharon. She was in the house so often these days she may as well have been living there—nobody had asked him if he minded—so he took it straight up to his room.

He flopped down onto his bed and tore the envelope open. Inside was a single white sheet, folded in two. He opened it and read the words. It was short and sweet:

Stop investigating or else.

TWENTY-FOUR

There was nothing else on the note. No further explanation. Brian's stomach churned with a mixture of fear and excitement. If someone was warning him off, then they must be closing in on something after all.

Who was it? And how did they know where he lived? He tried to think through the possibilities, but his head was spinning. He was certain Manuel and Bart, or whatever their names were, hadn't followed him. He'd surely have noticed them if they had. They weren't exactly the most subtle of guys.

Could it have been someone from the nursing home? Rodney hadn't known who Brian was—he was certain of that—but one of the old folks might have. And they could have told Rodney. They might not even have told him willingly. Rodney seemed like the sort of bully who could menace anyone into telling the truth.

What if the others had gotten a letter, too? He had to find out. He grabbed his phone, dialed Sam's number, and got the *no credit* message.

Brian leaped up and ran down the stairs, then remembered the letter, racing back to stuff it into his jeans pocket, before hurtling downstairs again. Within thirty seconds, he was on his bike, on his way to the twins' house as fast as he could. He skidded into corners, hanging so low he was almost scraping his knee on the ground at the turn. He wobbled a couple of times and once he had to swerve wildly to avoid a dog. The dog didn't seem to mind—he actually seemed to enjoy it, as he spent the next few hundred yards trying to keep up with Brian.

Brian jumped off his bike when he arrived at the twins' house. The bike continued moving along the sidewalk by itself before hitting a wall and crashing to the ground. Brian had already hopped over the gate and was around the back of the house where Adeyinka was playing a game with a couple of neighbors.

"Hi, Brian," she said sweetly, but there was no time for him to answer.

He leaped over the bags of recycling left behind from the previous night's party, wrenched open the back door, and dodged past Mrs. Adamu, then weaved around a couple of the twins' brothers, before running upstairs and bursting into Chris's room, too out of breath to talk. Chris was sitting on his bed, deep in thought, pages and pages of investigative notes spread all around him. He looked up, startled, as Brian handed him the envelope before collapsing in a heap on the carpet. Chris read the note.

"This is serious. We have to—"

"Not telling anyone," Brian wheezed. "Did you get one?"

"A letter? No," he said. "Don't think Sam did, either. I was talking to Hannah a few minutes ago and she didn't mention one. Let me check with Amelia."

"No, not yet. I want to . . . work this out. Tell me what . . . you think it means if I'm . . . the only one who got a letter."

"Possibly, that it's someone who knows you, but doesn't know us. Or else they only want to warn you specifically for some reason."

"Do you think that I'm the only one they're trying to warn?" Brian said, finally getting some of his breath back.

"I honestly don't know."

Brian hauled himself up onto the bed. His back was drenched with sweat and he needed a drink. He grabbed a carton of juice from the bedside table and tore it open, not even waiting to insert the straw. He chugged it all in one go before wiping his mouth clean with the back of his hand.

"We're in this investigation together, but I'm the only one who's gotten a warning," Brian said. "Even if I stopped, the rest of you would still continue trying to solve this, right?"

"Yes, almost certainly."

"So then why would they warn me? What's the point?"

"You're saying that taking you out of the equation wouldn't make much of a difference to the overall investigation? We'd still have a good chance of solving the crime whether you were there or not?"

"Exactly. You and Hannah are the brains. Sam is just as willing to step into certain danger as I am and Amelia . . . well, I don't know . . . Look, it makes no sense to only try to stop me, but not the rest of you."

Brian had a thought. Last night, outside the bathroom. It couldn't be . . . could it? She had been acting strangely.

"Do you have copies of the drawings?" he asked. "The drawings of the stuff that was in the attic in the cottage. Remember there were sketches of the stolen goods."

"Sure, yes. Hang on." Chris shuffled through the papers on the bed until he found what he was looking for. "Is this what you want?"

It was. The sketches of the painting, the lamp . . . and the necklace. The necklace he'd seen in Amelia's bag when she stumbled outside the bathroom at the party. He didn't want to believe it.

"What is it?" Chris asked.

"Give me a second. I need to think. She turns up, we go to the cottage, find the stuff. She's supposed to be looking after her grandmother, but there's nothing wrong with her. Nothing at all . . ."

Chris's face changed before Brian had time to continue. He knew the way his friend's brain worked—not always very well. "No, no, no. Tell me you don't . . . you don't suspect Amelia."

Brian held up the sketch of the necklace. "I don't want to suspect her, but last night at the party I saw this in her bag."

"And what did she say when you asked her about it?"

"What? I didn't ask her about it."

"Why not?"

"Why not? That doesn't matter. Look at the envelope. Look at how my name is spelled."

Even though he didn't want to, Chris did. *Bryan*. Brian spelled with a *Y*.

"She doesn't know how I spell my name. Everyone else does."

"But she's smart. *Brian* is the traditional spelling and if you're in doubt you'd go with the traditional spelling, wouldn't you?"

"Unless it was some kind of double-bluff. She might know I spell it *Brian*, so she spells it *Bryan* to stop us from suspecting her."

"Why would she do that?" Chris asked.

"She wants me out of the picture."

Chris's mouth dropped open with shock.

"Not dead! Maybe just not part of the Misfits Club."

"Brian, I love this club as much as you do, but the idea that someone is trying to break us up or something when we only have a short time left together anyway is ridiculous."

"All right, all right, that's probably a bit stupid," Brian admitted. "But, wait, I've got it."

He jumped off the bed and slapped his fist into the palm of his hand, a gesture that signified both anger and delight.

"What is it you've got?" Chris asked. He didn't think he wanted to hear it.

"It's a distraction. Amelia, the evil genius, set this whole thing up—the stolen goods, the haunted house, the whole thing. Think about it."

"I am thinking about it and it makes no sense."

"No, give it a minute. Nothing happens around here, right? Nothing exciting, I mean, before you say something happens everywhere."

"Go on," Chris said warily. He wondered if his friend had gone insane. It was possible. A lot had happened in Brian's life in the last couple of years and he never talked about it. Maybe bottling all that stuff up had been bad for him. Maybe today was the day he finally exploded.

"One day Amelia turns up. She tells Hannah she's staying with her grandmother because she's there to look after her. I've met Mrs. Parkinson—she does *not* need to be looked after. Definitely not."

Brian began pacing up and down the small bedroom.

"Amelia is suddenly friends with Hannah, even though she's been visiting Florence for years and never made an effort to meet Hannah before," he continued, "and somehow she gets us to agree to allow her to join the club. *She* picks the Ultimate Test card in Gravest Danger and it just happens to be the haunted-house card. Coincidence? I think not. We go to the cottage in the woods and that very day happens to be the day the stolen goods are there and Amelia *accidentally* photographs the man we haven't been able to find. We start looking for the goods, we find that the house is owned by Rodney. What if Rodney is just there to distract people from the truth of what's happening?"

"You think that some adults think the Misfits Club is so dangerous and so good at investigating that they want us distracted from whatever secret scheme they're actually operating?"

"Er, yeah. Something like that. I haven't worked out all the details yet."

Chris threw his hands up in the air. He'd never heard such nonsense in his life. "Who? Who is the mastermind behind all of this?"

Brian hadn't thought that far ahead. "Amelia's dad? Maybe Manuel or Bart is Amelia's father."

"We've seen her father. Driving past when they visit, remember? He looks nothing like Manuel or Bart."

"Maybe they're her uncles or something. Listen to me. She has the necklace in her bag. Why would she have it if she didn't steal it? And who else could have delivered the note to my house? Who even knows we're investigating? My dad? Your dad? It wasn't Manuel or Bart because they don't seem like gentle note-writing kind of guys, do they?"

"Right, that's it. I've had enough. Come with me."

Chris put his tablet into his backpack and slipped it over

his shoulders. He left the room and was halfway down the stairs when Brian caught up with him.

"Where are we going?" Brian asked.

Chris stopped to face his friend. "We're going to talk to Amelia."

"But—"

"No *buts*. Nothing. The Misfits Club is not a place for secrets and you're right—Mrs. Parkinson *doesn't* need looking after. So we're going to ask her what she's really doing here and she's going to tell us and maybe then you'll stop making up crazy theories."

"You'll give the game away. If she's trying to trick us—"

"Then she'll know we're onto her. If she's as much of a genius as you say, and has set all of this up, then she's going to be ten steps ahead of us anyway, so we may as well put our cards on the table."

They met Sam coming in the door as they were on their way out of the house.

"We're off to meet Amelia," Chris said.

"I'll come with you. What's going on?"

"Brian thinks that Amelia might be the brains behind the whole stolen-treasure thing and is using the Misfits Club to complete some dastardly scheme that's been set in motion, probably by the criminal we mistook for a poltergeist. Oh, and he thinks the criminal might be Amelia's father. We're going to confront her about it."

Sam grabbed his bike and hopped on. He wheelied his way to the sidewalk outside his house.

"Aren't you surprised? Don't you have any questions?" Brian asked.

"No and no," Sam said.

"Oh, okay. You suspect her, too?"

"Absolutely not. Not even for a second. I just want to see you make a fool of yourself."

A summer breeze had picked up, cooling the muggy afternoon air. The street was filled with the noise of trimmers and lawn mowers as people took advantage of the good weather to do some gardening. As the three of them biked down the road, Brian wondered if he'd just made a huge mistake.

TWENTY-FIVE

"The Five Find-Outers and Dog never made things this complicated for themselves," Hannah said.

"Maybe the dog calmed them all down and made them less stupid," Chris said, looking pointedly at Brian.

They were all gathered in Hannah's other garden shed, which was hot and cramped and uncomfortable. She didn't dare risk going to their much cozier club headquarters, just in case her mother returned early. Hannah had given Amelia the best seat, which was on the riding lawn mower. Hannah was sitting on an upturned bucket while Chris was perched on the top of an aluminum stepladder. Brian and Sam had decided to stand.

Hannah's mother had gone into town while her father had just returned from a five-mile run. He'd gone for a shave and a shower so Hannah had snuck out of the house. Unfortunately for Hannah, he'd hidden his laptop so she still hadn't had the opportunity to access it, which was driving her nuts. She'd managed to solve her mobile-phone problem, though. She'd taken out the SIM card before it had been confiscated and had switched it into an old phone with a cracked screen that she'd found in a kitchen drawer. She reckoned they had about fifteen minutes before her dad would notice she was missing.

"What's this all about?" Amelia asked.

"To be blunt, it's about you," Chris said.

He took out the letter and handed it to Amelia.

"This is addressed to Brian," she said.

Brian was monitoring her reactions closely. "It's all right—you can read it."

She opened the letter and read the contents. Her face turned pale. Either she was a fantastic actor or Brian had been wrong about her.

"Did you get a letter like that?" Chris asked.

"No, I didn't," Amelia said.

She looked both worried and confused.

"None of us did," Hannah said.

"Who do you think wrote it?"

"We have no idea," Chris said. He looked over to Brian. "We should draw up a list of suspects and . . ."

Amelia noticed Brian wasn't looking at her. His head was down, as if he couldn't bring himself to look up in case he caught her eye. And then it dawned on her.

"Wait a second," she said.

The other Misfits suddenly found their feet very interesting, too. She'd figured it out. She really had. She was smart, all right.

"You don't think *I* wrote this, do you?" Amelia asked.

"Yes," Brian said.

"But why would I do something as sneaky as that?"

"I don't know, Amelia. Why would you have a stolen necklace in your bag? A necklace that was once in the attic in the cottage in the woods."

Sam gasped. "Sorry, that was far too dramatic. Carry on."

"I found it," Amelia said.

"You found the necklace? Really? And where did you find it?"

"At the party last night. At Sam and Chris's house."

"And you expect me to believe that? If you found it, why didn't you tell anyone?"

"I did. I told Hannah."

Brian turned to Hannah. "Did—"

"Yes, she did. I was about to tell you this morning when my mother came into the room and I started singing. We decided to wait until we were all together to talk about it."

"Oh."

That changed things quite a bit.

"So you thought I was in on it? That *I* was one of the thieves?" Amelia said.

"Yes."

"But why? Why would you think that?"

Brian stuck his chin in the air and looked her squarely in the eye.

"Okay, well . . . first of all, you told us you came here to look after your grandmother. She *does not* need someone to take care of her. She's really healthy and strong. I saw the way she swung that sledgehammer."

"That's it?" Hannah said.

"No, there's more," Brian said.

He was starting to feel uncomfortable. It had all made sense when the adrenaline was flowing and he was shouting his suspicions at Chris. Now that he was calmer, it sounded, well, a lot more feeble.

"And I saw you on the couch last night. You smiled at me."

Hannah tried to suppress a smile of her own. "That *does* sound like a criminal thing to do. If you smile, you're definitely guilty."

"Shut up," Brian said. "It was a strange smile, all right. Like you were up to something."

"Was that after I broke the plates? When I sat on the couch?" Amelia asked.

"Yes."

"That's when I discovered the necklace. It was stuffed under one of the cushions. I was excited, but I didn't want to let anyone know. I tried to look as normal as I could. Guess I failed. Was there anything else, Brian?"

"Yes. No?" Brian was confused now. She had an answer for every question. "Wait, there was—something else I had to say, about . . . you and your family being . . . evil geniuses . . ."

To everyone's surprise, Amelia didn't storm off or sulk or shout or throw something. Chris assumed she'd be extremely insulted by the accusation, which is why it took him a moment to realize she was laughing. Her whole body shook and then fat tears of laughter rolled down her face. None of them had ever seen her like this. They'd barely seen her crack a smile before.

"You're an idiot, Brian," she said. "You really are an idiot."

His great big theory sounded so stupid now. He *was* an idiot. "I know, I—"

"I mean, you—you—you . . . heeeee, thought I—"

She leaned forward over the steering wheel of the lawn mower, trying and failing to control herself.

"I told him he was being a moron," Chris said.

"Why? I mean . . . heeee . . . what reason would I have for . . . heee."

"All right, I might have gotten it wrong. Can we just move on from it?" Brian said. The back of his neck was tingling with the embarrassment of it all.

"We will for now," Hannah said, "but we'll come back to it later. We're not going to forget this in a hurry."

"Wait," Chris said. "Are we sure it's the same necklace?"

Amelia got to her feet and grabbed her bag, still chuckling a little. She unzipped it and took out the necklace. It was a definite match for the one in the sketch.

"I remember it from the attic," Hannah said. "What about you, Sam?"

"All necklaces look the same to me."

"Okay, so if Amelia found it at the party, then that

means someone at the party was involved. Since those Manuel and Bart characters weren't there . . ." Chris began.

"It means we're not just looking for two people, we're definitely looking for three," Hannah said.

Brian hadn't heard what anybody had said in the last couple of minutes. He was feeling bad. Yes, Amelia was right. There was no doubt about it—he was a first-class idiot.

"Look, I messed up. I'm sorry, Amelia. I really am."

"It's okay," Amelia said.

"It's okay?"

"It's partly my fault. I haven't been completely honest and you probably sensed that."

"I . . . What now?"

"I didn't want to come to Newpark and I didn't want to join your club because I thought it was stupid, but I was wrong. As wrong as you were about me."

"You don't have to tell them," Hannah said.

"I know, but I'd like to." She looked around the garden shed at the faces of the other Misfits. "I'm not here to look after my gran. You're right, she's totally able to look after herself and, even if she wasn't, she wouldn't let anyone mind her. The truth is I have a new baby sister. I thought she was the really annoying one, but it turns out *I* was annoying everybody else. I, you know, might have complained about my sister crying all the time and I didn't really help around the house. They'd probably have put up with it, but then I did something a little bit stupid and my dad decided that we needed a break from each other."

"What was the stupid thing?" Sam asked.

"I hoped you wouldn't ask. My stepmother, Vivienne, was always trying to get me to relax more. She said I was too uptight."

"You? Never."

"I don't believe it for a second," Hannah said, smiling.

"Mock if you want, Hannah, but I'm not the one hiding in a garden shed because I'm scared of my parents."

"I'm not hiding! I chose to be here. And I'm not scared of my parents. Not even a little bit," Hannah said, remembering to check the time on her mobile phone when she thought nobody was looking. Still two minutes left before she needed to go back in.

"Anyway, it was fun before because we used to do all this stuff together, but then she said she couldn't do anything with me because she was pregnant, and then the baby was born. Vivienne and Dad argued forever over the baby name and they finally decided on Susanna. The name was this whole big thing with them. I went with Vivienne to register the birth.

"You have to fill out these forms and then this person on a computer prints off a birth certificate. Susanna started crying—she cries all the time—and so I said I'd hand in the forms for her while Vivienne took her outside. Before I handed them in, I decided, for a joke, to change the name on the form. The guy who registered the birth was a bit surprised, but he said he was seeing all sorts of weird baby names these days, so he went ahead with it. I got the certificate, but Vivienne was so distracted by my sister that she didn't even look at it. Nobody checked until later on when Dad came home from work and they asked to see it. When they saw it, they went through the roof."

"What did you change the name to?"

"Supergirl."

"What?" Brian asked.

"Yeah, Supergirl Princess Parkinson. Well, they were always saying how great she was and calling her a princess and all that, so I thought, if you think she's super, then why not just call her Supergirl? I thought it was a silly joke, but they didn't agree."

"Does she have to be called Supergirl forever, like when she goes to school?" Sam asked.

"No, they changed it back. But they got really angry and I ended up here."

"You're no Trick Whittington, but you're definitely in the right club—you're a hundred percent Misfit," Sam said.

"Oh yeah, a complete Misfit," Brian said. "There's something else, Amelia—I didn't want you in the club. Not because I didn't like you, but because I wanted things to stay the way they were. I was wrong about that, too."

"I don't want to go to Galway," Chris said.

"What?" Hannah said.

"Since we're sharing stuff. I like it here. I've always liked it here. It's home and I like living a two-minute walk from the countryside and I like my friends and I don't want to go. I hate the idea of the club breaking up and I didn't say anything because I didn't want to upset anyone. My mom's really looking forward to it."

"I'm kind of looking forward to it, too," Sam said. "Moving to the city *is* exciting. But I'll miss this, man. I'll really miss this."

"This?"

"Yeah, hanging around, talking nonsense, and acting stupid like dopey old Brian there. All that stuff. It's fun, right?"

Everyone sat or stood in silence for a moment.

"Are we finished with the emotional talk because it's really creeping me out," Hannah said to break the tension.

Brian laughed. "Almost. Look, we don't have to like what's happening—you guys moving away and all that—but we're not finished yet. There's a mystery to solve. We're going to solve it because we want to stop a bunch of criminals from doing criminal things, we're going to solve it to show our parents that they're wrong, and we're going to solve it because it's going to be the last and best thing the Misfits Club will ever do."

Chris gave Brian a pat on the shoulder while Amelia and Sam fist-bumped and shared high fives with Hannah.

"Right, now that that's over, we can get back to work,"

Hannah said. "If you don't believe Amelia was the one who sent you that letter, who do you think it was?"

"I don't know. It has to be someone who knows where I live, so that doesn't really narrow it down. Most of the people at the party know where I live."

"It might not be safe for you to stay at home," Chris said. "You should crash at our house until we've got all of this figured out."

"Definitely," Sam said.

"I know Gran would put you up, too. She's got a spare room and an air mattress. You wouldn't even have to give her a reason," Amelia said.

"Thanks, but I'll be fine. I'm not running away. Anyway, someone has to keep an eye on Mucky."

"Won't Sharon do that?" Amelia asked.

Too late, she noticed the others shaking their heads and drawing their fingers across their throats in order to get her to be quiet.

"I think Sharon worries more about herself than she does my dad these days. She's not very nice to him," Brian said.

Sam looked for a subtle way to quickly change the subject. He couldn't find one, so he said the first thing that came into his head.

"My teacher described me as perennially useless, but I wasn't sure what he meant," he said.

"You hardly thought it was a good thing," Chris said, playing along.

"I was willing to be optimistic," Sam said. "Okay, now that—"

Hannah checked her phone. She was running late again. "My time's up!"

She ran from the shed and straight into her house, leaving the others behind.

"Do we just stay here or what?" Sam asked.

"No," Amelia said. "Now it's time to blow this case wide open."

The others stared at her.

"Sorry, I saw that on a detective show once and I've always wanted to say it."

"Wish you hadn't said it. Makes you a little less cool. And you'd already lost a lot of cool points over the Supergirl story," Sam said. "So, are we going to check out that farmhouse now, or what?"

"Definitely," Brian said. "Let's rock 'n' roll."

"I think that's worse," Sam said.

"Really? My dad says it all the time," Brian said. "No, you're right. That *is* worse."

TWENTY-SIX

After Hannah had gone, the others prepared for action. Despite Chris wanting to get back to work on his computer, Amelia persuaded him to go with them. She told him that they hadn't had a successful morning checking out the two houses and that, with his intelligence, he might spot something that they hadn't. Her attempt at flattery worked. What she didn't explain was that they needed his lock-picking skills and that Sam had brought along his brother's lock-picking set. She didn't want to spook him just yet.

They packed their backpacks with all the supplies they thought they'd need, including flashlights, mobile phones, screwdrivers, chips, chocolate, and soda. They were biking down a quiet country road on the way to the farmhouse when Amelia's phone rang. It was Hannah.

She was still disgusted at the thought of being trapped at home rather than being on the road with the rest of the gang, but they knew it was the best thing to do. If she snuck out and her parents discovered she was missing—and they would—they'd start looking for her and they wouldn't stop until they'd located her. If they didn't find her in the first hour, they'd get the authorities involved and if they were looking for the Misfits, there'd be no chance of completing the investigation.

Amelia got them all to pull over to the side of the road, waited until Chris had caught up with them, and then put Hannah on speakerphone.

"It's only a matter of time before my folks realize I have a phone, so listen up," she said.

Despite the remote location, the phone signal was good and her voice was loud and clear.

"I got out of going to Mrs. Finnegan's by faking illness and Dad felt sorry for me and gave me his laptop. Mom would never have given in like that. Anyway, I've had a breakthrough. Those art-analyst guys I contacted online got back to me. They recognized the painting."

Chris brought out a copy of the sketch Amelia had drawn of the painting in the attic.

"It's called *Foundering* and it's by a guy called Duven Klempst. It was stolen from a museum in Amsterdam earlier this year. Guess what it's worth?"

There was silence.

"Seventy-five thousand euro. That's a lot, but there were other paintings in that museum that were just as easy to steal and were worth a lot more. There had to be a reason they stole *that* painting. And then I remembered something like this had happened in one of my detective books."

"Hang on. Could they be stealing things to order?" Chris asked.

"That's what I think, Chris. It's in *The Dead Man's Twist*. Criminals get a shopping list from some rich guys and they only steal what the rich guys want. They leave behind everything else no matter what it's worth," Hannah said.

This was exactly the kind of thing that drove Sam nuts.

"Dumb it down for me, guys," he said.

Brian was glad he'd said that. He was having trouble following things as well.

"Say you have a lot of money," Hannah replied, "and you'd like to buy a painting or an antique piece of jewelry or something, but the person who owns it doesn't want to sell it, what do you do?"

"Give up," Brian said.

"Yeah, that's what a normal person would do, but some people don't give in that easily—rich people. Like, say a rich guy wants the *Mona Lisa*, he tells a criminal and he goes to that museum in Paris and steals it. Then the rich guy pays him for stealing it. The criminal doesn't have to go around looking for someone to buy the stuff he's stolen like a regular burglar," Hannah explained. "It's already arranged beforehand, so it's neat and tidy. It's only a guess, but that's what I think."

Sam whistled in admiration.

"I also got in touch with Horace," she continued. "He

told me that the man who owns the farmhouse you're heading to is called Frederick O'Callaghan."

"Does he live there?" Brian asked.

"He doesn't live at all. He's dead, but his daughter, who lives in New Zealand, is renting it out. My guess is she's renting it to our criminal friends."

"So that's where we're heading for right now," Sam said, hopping back on his bike.

"Wait," Chris said. "We haven't come up with a plan."

"There's been too much talking and I'm sick of plans," Sam said. "Let's just go there and see what happens."

And, with that, he was off, pedaling furiously.

"I don't know what's in the house," Hannah said over the phone as the others got on their bikes, "but, if my theory is correct, it could be anything the criminals are able to sell."

Brian didn't bother to respond. He slung his backpack over his shoulders, slipped the bike into first gear, and followed Sam down the road.

Amelia thanked Hannah for her hard work, said goodbye, and ended the call.

"I guess it's up to you and me to formulate a plan, Am—" Chris began.

"Try and keep up with us this time," Amelia said as she took off after Sam and Brian.

"Come on!" Sam shouted. He'd twisted around to see

where his brother was and now he was turned backward while riding forward.

"He's not even keeping his eyes on the road. How can we possibly be related?" Chris said. He pressed his foot on the pedal and shouted back. "Wait for me."

TWENTY-SEVEN

"Absolutely not. No way. Not going to happen. I am not picking the lock, no matter what you say," Chris said.

They were back at the place that Brian and Sam had now visited twice, once when trapped in the trunk of the car. To Chris's eyes, it was just as bleak and lonely as they'd described it—all empty outhouses, discarded farm equipment, and silence. At 6:56 p.m., four members of the Misfits Club had biked into the yard of the remote farmhouse.

"Kind of eerie around here," Chris said.

Sam agreed. "The sort of place where you could scream and scream and nobody would ever hear you. Are we just going to stand around or are we actually going to do something?"

"I'm not going to pick the lock," Chris said.

"But I made a big speech back in the shed," Brian said. "About the club and doing it for us and lots of other stuff that I forget now, but it was a really good speech. You have to do it."

Chris folded his arms tightly in a gesture of defiance. He

was upset. He hadn't even realized that they'd brought along his lock-picking kit until Sam produced it.

"I don't want you to pick the lock," Amelia said.

"You don't?" Brian said.

Chris looked at her as if he didn't quite believe it.

"No, I want you to teach me how to do it," she said.

"I don't know . . . that sounds—"

"Didn't you promise to investigate crime, fight evil, and put yourself in peril to right wrongdoings everywhere?" Amelia said. "Forget Brian's speech—that's the Misfits Club promise."

"You're using my own words against me?" Chris said.

"Yes, I learned them by heart. They're nice words, but unless you actually do what they say they mean nothing."

Chris thought about it. Those words *did* mean something to him. Was he breaking the law if he—

"Oh, for the love of . . . for once in your life, stop thinking and *do* something," Sam cried. "Why did you even bother to learn how to pick a lock if you think it's wrong to pick a lock? It makes no sense."

"I'd just have to show you how to do it?" Chris said to Amelia.

"That's all. But we really need to get going. I mean if Manuel and Bart turn up, and you've just been wasting time thinking about things—"

"Okay, okay, let's start."

It turned out that lock-picking wasn't a skill that was

easily taught. Amelia did her best, but it wasn't working out. The more Chris spoke, doing his best to guide her through, the more irritated she became. He was standing too close to her, just over her shoulder, blocking her light and generally annoying her with his presence.

Sam was wandering around the perimeter of the house, checking again and again for another point of entry, but he hadn't had any luck. Brian wasn't much happier. When they'd arrived, he'd imagined that they'd pick the lock, get in, and find the goods—whatever they might be—but here he was, just hanging around like an idiot. He'd had more fun waiting for a bus. His thoughts turned to the letter. Who could have sent it? He took it from his pocket and read it again. *Stop investigating or else.* Or else what?

He could guess.

"You're not doing it right. You have to . . . no, it has to be a more delicate touch than that, Amelia. You have to . . ."

Brian walked back to the milking shed, checking that the bikes were well hidden for at least the third time. What was taking Chris and Amelia so long?

"Oh, for goodness' sake. You're such a know-it-all, Chris," Amelia said.

"Know-it-all? Know-it-all? If you just listened to me, we'd be in by now."

"You make out that it's so easy. If it's so easy, then why don't you show me how it's done?" Amelia said.

She flung the tools on the ground and stormed off across the yard.

"I *will* show you," Chris huffed.

He picked the gadgets up and began working on the lock immediately. Amelia joined Brian, who was smirking. He'd been dealing with Chris's perfectionist ways for years.

"See how annoying he can be?" Brian said.

"Is he picking the lock?" Amelia asked. Her back was to the farmhouse.

"Yeah, he is."

"See, I told you I'd persuade him to do it."

"But . . . you mean, you tricked him into . . ."

Amelia didn't reply. She just smiled.

"Well done, Chris," Sam said, less than five minutes later.

The front door was open. They were in. Chris stood in the doorway, looking smug.

"See, told you it was easy," he said.

"You were right," Amelia said. "Sorry I doubted you."

"Oh, well, don't worry about . . . I, er . . . It's all forgotten. Let's go in."

When Sam and Brian had finished slapping him on the back, hoping the praise would be enough to make him forget that he didn't want to do what he'd just done, the four of them stepped into the filthy old hallway.

The last thing Chris wanted was to go into the house. Apart from the possibility of infections and dirt, there was also the chance of severe injury or death. He'd told them all a thousand times before that venturing into creepy houses was likely to end badly, but it was too silent outside. Far too silent to stay out there by himself, so he followed them in and pulled the front door shut behind him.

TWENTY-EIGHT

Alex Lambert, the ringleader of the thieves, Lionel and Burt's boss, didn't like the person on the other end of the telephone. Lambert considered him to be obnoxious, but, unfortunately, when it came to doing business like this, you often had to deal with obnoxious people.

Cornelius Figg, Ireland's richest man, had been shouting down the telephone since he'd grabbed it from Plunkett Healy almost two minutes earlier.

"This was supposed to have been delivered by now," Figg roared. "My Barney is practically in tears."

"Please don't use any names, one-five-four-two. There's been a delay, but we'll have it to you in a couple of hours."

Lambert didn't like it when people lost their tempers. It showed a lack of control, and when you were out of control you made mistakes.

"Make sure that it is. I've put a lot of money your way over the years, but that gravy train will come to a stop if you mess this up."

"It'll be delivered."

Figg's temper ran out of steam. "Is it, you know, dangerous?"

What do you think? Lambert felt like saying.

"One of my workers almost lost a hand."

"Right, good. Dangerous enough, then," Figg said. He seemed thoughtful for a moment, before his anger boiled up again. "Do what you're paid to do and do it properly."

Lambert ended the call.

"Who was that?" Lionel asked.

I'm working with morons, Lambert thought. A smarter man than Lionel—which, in Lambert's opinion, was nearly every man who had ever existed—would have realized that it had to be Cornelius Figg on the phone. Lionel needed everything explained to him.

There were only two positive things that Lambert could say about Lionel. The first was that he was smarter than his brother, Burt. Not much of an achievement, admittedly, since Burt had once been outsmarted by a fly. He'd been trying to kill the insect when it had escaped through a window. Burt had followed it, forgetting his apartment was on the second floor, and had plummeted to the ground, breaking both ankles and his left arm. The fly was unharmed. The second positive thing was that Lionel and indeed Burt were extremely loyal. They'd always do what they were told to do and they rarely questioned orders. They didn't always understand them, but they rarely questioned them.

"Where's Burt?" Lambert asked.

"BUUUURRRRTTTT," Lionel roared.

Lambert smacked Lionel across the back of his head. "I could have done that myself."

"Aaarggh," Lionel yelped. "That hurt."

Lambert hadn't seen Lionel and Burt for years, not until a sudden move back to Ireland six months earlier. Prior to that, Alex Lambert had been working in the United States until the Nevada police force had uncovered the illegal import-and-export business Alex had been running.

The business had clients in Ireland, making it a good choice of location to restart the operation. After coming so close to being arrested, Lambert no longer trusted former colleagues, so had decided to work with family instead. Lambert's brothers—Lionel and Burt—collected and transported stolen items to and from rented properties. Since Lambert hadn't been home for a long time, finding the right properties in which to store the items had been difficult. The cottage in the woods? Paying money to that whining senior citizen in the nursing home? That had been a foolish mistake.

"Is everything ready?" Alex Lambert asked.

"The trailer's on the back of the Impreza. We're good to go," Lionel Lambert replied.

"The Impreza. What have I told you about finding a low-key vehicle? The last thing we need is to attract attention."

"The Impreza's cool. Anyway, we're in a rush now."

"This is the last time you're driving it. Understood?"

"Yes, Alex."

Burt arrived in the room munching on a burger that he held in his bandaged left hand. He seemed oblivious to the river of burger juice that dribbled down his chin as it rushed to join the delta of melted cheese and tomato-sauce stains on the front of his Pantera T-shirt.

"Aren't you fat enough already?" Alex Lambert asked.

For a moment, it looked as if Burt was about to cry. "I'm actually the right weight for my height," he said.

"Yeah, if you were seven foot three," Lionel chuckled.

"Throw that burger in the trash," Alex Lambert said to Burt.

Burt threw the burger in the garbage can, occasionally looking back at it longingly.

"And you, Lionel, stop making stupid jokes. We have work to do. The buyer is meeting us later on tonight. Just off the Galway road. We need to pack up the item he's purchasing."

"How much is he paying?" Lionel asked.

"Well, if—"

Alex Lambert stopped when the smartphone buzzed into life.

The look on Lambert's face was one the brothers had seen before when they were kids and had hoped never to see again.

Lionel finally summoned up the nerve to ask. "What's wrong?"

"The silent alarm at the farmhouse has been set off. Go there now. I'll follow you shortly," Lambert said. "And make sure you don't let whoever's in there get away. No excuses this time."

"Don't worry, we won't let you down," Burt said.

"We'll do whatever it takes," Lionel said, pounding his fist into the palm of his hand.

TWENTY-NINE

As Chris shut the front door behind him, he was hit by the smell. He took out a tissue and covered his mouth and nose.

"That's terrible. It smells like . . . like . . ."

"Poop?" Sam said.

"Yes, exactly like that," Chris agreed.

"That's what I thought, too," Brian said.

"Maybe they're just not very house-proud," Amelia suggested. Like Chris, she too was covering her nose and mouth.

"Not being very house-proud means a bit of untidiness—it doesn't mean an overwhelming smell of poop," Chris said.

"Can we stop discussing smells? We said we'd get in and out of here quickly. Let's stick to that," Brian said.

"He's right," Amelia said. "Chris and me will check out the ground floor. Sam and Brian, you go upstairs. Agreed?"

Brian and Sam headed up the stairs. The banister was greasy and grimy. There wasn't a bulb in any of the light fixtures, so they used their flashlights to pick their way through the gloom. The smell was stronger up here, a lot stronger.

"It's horrible," Sam said as his flashlight picked out faded and torn wallpaper. "It's like—I don't know what it's like. I feel a bit sick."

There were three rooms upstairs. The nearest was on Brian's left, just off the landing. The other two were at the far end of the hall, one on either side, the doors opposite each other.

Brian nodded at the door closest to him. "This one first?"

He thought Sam was going to go in with him, but his friend continued down the corridor, sniffing the air and talking to himself until he was standing between the two doors at the far end of the hall. The room on Sam's left overlooked the wild garden at the back of the house, the one on his right, the farmyard at the front.

Brian took a deep breath as his hand gripped the brass handle. It was cold to the touch. He slowly twisted it until he heard a click. He pushed the door open and then stepped inside.

Even though the room was dominated by an ornate fireplace, it was cold in there. The patterned wallpaper was faded and it looked as if someone had once begun the job of peeling it off, but had given up before they'd even reached the halfway point. Apart from two large wooden crates by the fireplace, the room was empty.

Brian shone the flashlight into the corners to make sure

he wasn't missing anything. When he'd convinced himself that he wasn't, he walked over to the crates. They were as tall as he was and were sealed shut. They had no markings and no obvious lock or fastenings. A quick examination of each one led him to the same conclusion—they'd need a crowbar to open them. He couldn't remember if someone had brought one along. There had been so much stuff packed into their backpacks that it was difficult to remember everything.

He was about to call for Chris when he heard the shout.

"Sam," he cried out.

It was Sam's voice he'd heard, all right—just down the narrow hallway. His own shout brought the others running. Sam was standing outside the door on the left at the far end of the hall. He was completely still, an unreadable expression on his face.

"Sam, what is it? Are you hurt? What happened?"

His friend's eyes were wide, his pupils huge. He didn't look injured. He kept staring at the door.

"Are you okay?" Amelia called out.

"Stay where you are," Brian shouted at them. "Something's wrong. I don't know what yet. Just . . . just stay there." He lowered his voice. "Sam? Talk to me."

"I'm not hurt," Sam said.

"What's wrong, then?"

Sam slowly turned his head until he was facing his friend. He looked him directly in the eyes.

"Have a look in there and tell me what you see."

Brian pushed the door open. The stench that rushed out to meet him was almost overwhelming. He gagged a few times before he managed to control his breathing. There was nothing in the room apart from a single crate. At first glance, it looked like the crates he'd found in the other room, but as he got closer he saw that there were some differences. There was a small, clear, square window in the center of one of the panels. There were holes in the top—seven small circles, an inch in diameter, punched through the wood. And there were five bolts across the front panel. Whatever was in there was meant to stay in there.

He could hear something moving inside, scratching at the wood, something that sounded like it had claws.

Was that a growl?

Brian leaned down and pressed his face against the window.

Something flew forward and smacked against the plastic in flash of black and white and sharp pointed teeth.

Brian toppled over backward, letting out an involuntary swearword. His heart was racing. What *was* that?

"Brian?" Amelia called.

"I'm okay, I'm okay." At least, he thought he was.

Chris and Amelia raced down the hall and joined them in the room. Their eyes widened when the smell hit and it took them a moment to compose themselves.

"What did you see?" Amelia asked, holding her nose.

He wasn't sure.

"Some kind of animal, I think," he replied.

"You think?"

"It . . . well," Sam said, "I know this sounds crazy, but it looks like . . . a really muscly skunk. Like one that's drunk a ton of protein shakes and then gone down to the gym every day for a year and . . . let me look again."

He shoved Brian out of the way and leaned forward until his nose was almost touching the plastic window. The crate shook as the creature leaped forward again.

"Yeeee," Sam yelped as he dived to his left, landing awkwardly on the wooden floor. He got to his feet. His hands were trembling. He stuffed them in his pockets so nobody would notice. "Okay, whatever's in that crate is absolutely insane."

"Chris, you're the animal expert, right?" Amelia said. "Why don't you have a look?"

"No offense, Amelia, but if myself and Brian can't handle it, I don't think Chris is going to be any use. There's something seriously wrong with that skunk."

Brian nodded his agreement.

"I think I'll give it a try all the same," Chris said.

He strode across the room, then got down on his haunches until he, too, was peering in through the smeary window. The moment he did, the animal leaped forward again, battering the panel. Unlike the others, Chris didn't move. Instead a slow smile spread across his face.

"Oh my gosh, if you aren't the cutest little thing I ever saw," he said.

The crate shook again.

"Chris, get out of there before it escapes and eats you."

"I'm fine," Chris said. He turned to the others. "It's not a skunk. It's a honey badger. From Africa."

Sam started laughing. "For a moment there, I thought you said it was a badger."

"I did say it was a badger."

"You're not thinking straight. Whatever's in there is vicious and dangerous and badgers are nonthreatening and cuddly and—"

"No, you're wrong, Sam. I saw a program on honey badgers before," Amelia said. "They're kind of tough."

"They're more than tough. They're super-intelligent and strong and they're not afraid of *anything*," Chris said. "They're one of the coolest creatures on the planet."

"Really? You think a badger's cool?"

"They'll even take on lions in a fight," Chris said. "Would you take on a lion?"

"Depends on the lion," Sam said. "All right, all right, I wouldn't."

Even though he could see it, Chris could hardly believe it. A honey badger. Right here. In a crate. In a farmhouse.

In Newpark. He looked into the crate again. It seemed to have calmed down. It was sitting on a bed of straw, staring out at him.

It looks sad, he thought.

It was about three feet long and had black fur, with a thick gray-white stripe running from its eyeline to its tail. Now it was on the move again, scurrying forward.

It slammed against the inside of the crate once more, shifting the entire thing forward another few inches.

"It really is strong," Amelia said.

"And it's got these huge long claws and its skin can stop bullets and . . ."

Chris stopped talking. "And what, Chris?"

"And it shouldn't be here," he said.

"So, I guess when Hannah said she thought these criminals were trading in rare items, one of those items turned out to be exotic pets."

"Looks like it, Sam," Amelia said.

"Remember all that hair that was stuck to my T-shirt from the blanket that time we were trapped in the trunk of the car? I think we know where that came from now. It wasn't a dog, after all," Sam said.

"Nope, not a dog. It was a honey badger. Why would anyone want a honey badger?" Brian asked.

Chris didn't look right. For a moment, they thought he might be having a panic attack. The change had come over him all of a sudden. None of them had ever seen him like this before. His nostrils flared, his jaw clenched, and he looked as if he wanted to hit someone. Chris had never wanted to hit someone in his life.

"So they could sell it. Because they're money-grabbing, inconsiderate fools," Chris said. "They've taken this beautiful creature—"

Sam raised his eyebrows at that. The honey badger looked more scary than beautiful to him.

"—from its natural environment so that some idiot can keep it as a pet? That's not right."

"It's terrible, but, unfortunately, it happens all over the world," Amelia said.

"Well, it won't happen here," Chris said.

"I still don't get it—why would anyone want a honey badger as a pet? I mean, I know people keep tigers and snakes and stuff, but a badger?"

"We'll figure that out later. You three go downstairs," Chris said. "Call Debra. And don't give me a reason as to why you don't want to call her. Just call her. And do it now. Is that clear?"

He said it so firmly, so authoritatively, that the others felt compelled to obey him.

"Absolutely, no problem. We'll do that," Brian said. "Are you going to be okay up here?"

He knew how fond Chris was of animals and he didn't want him doing anything foolish.

Chris turned to him. "Just do as I say, Brian."

"Okey-doke, I think my brother has gone to a weird place, but I also think he's right. This one needs the police," Sam said. "We're going downstairs now, Chris. Promise me you won't let that thing out."

"How stupid do you think I am?"

Brian, Amelia, and Sam stumbled down the stairs. Nobody's legs seemed to be working properly. Chris unslung his backpack from his shoulder and opened it up. He'd find what he was looking for in there. He was annoyed when he heard the footsteps on the landing.

"What are you doing back here?" Chris asked.

His three friends had just come back up the stairs. "We've got a problem," Sam said.

He'd been just about to call Debra O'Loughlin when the Subaru Impreza roared into the yard.

THIRTY

Brian looked out the upstairs window to the yard below as the car skidded to a halt, the trailer hitched to the back of it swinging wide as Lionel made a handbrake turn.

"Anyone got any ideas, other than panicking wildly?" Amelia asked.

"Sam and Brian, get that front door locked quickly, then shove something heavy up against it," Chris said.

They were on it immediately, bounding down the stairs two at a time.

"That won't be enough to keep them out, will it?" Amelia asked.

"I just need to buy us a few minutes," Chris said.

When Lionel spotted Sam, he sprinted across the yard and shoulder-charged the door. Sam got it locked, just in time. Lionel hit the door with such force it shook on its hinges, but it held fast.

Brian was in the kitchen, pushing against a grimy old white fridge. It toppled over with a *whoomph* that was followed by a muffled metallic clang as it hit the ground.

Sam's joy at locking the door was ended almost

immediately when he saw that Burt had a bunch of keys in his hand. He was searching for the right one.

"I need help," Brian called.

Sam joined Brian, and the two of them pushed the fridge—which was now lying on its side—along the floor. It was heavy, but a surge of adrenaline gave them a sudden burst of strength and energy. The moving fridge dug a groove in the linoleum, but they made it into the hall and up to the door, just as Burt unlocked it and began to push his way in.

The fridge was enough to block the door from being opened any farther. There was a gap between the door and frame now, about eight inches, but it wasn't enough to accommodate Burt's bulk. He managed to get his foot through the gap and on top of the fridge, but he couldn't haul the rest of himself through.

Brian and Sam kept their shoulders low, shoving the fridge against the door, trying desperately to close it, but Burt was pushing back. And Lionel was pushing Burt. Together, they were stronger than the two young Misfits. If the fridge hadn't worked as a kind of wedge, they'd have been in the house already.

"Guys?" Brian shouted.

"Keep them out for as long as you can," Amelia roared down the stairs. She turned to Chris. "Will this work?"

"I haven't a clue," he said. "I hope so."

They'd crossed the hall to the room that overlooked the

farmyard. The room had been painted a shockingly bright blue. They both had screwdrivers in their hands and they were unscrewing the lock on the door. Chris looked over his shoulder. He'd left the door of the room on the other side of the hall open and he could see the honey badger's crate. He could hear it moving around in there. It was restless and they were anxious.

"It's not going to be able to get out of there, is it?" Amelia asked.

"They're able to use tools to escape. I've seen a documentary where they worked as a team to open gates."

"That doesn't make me any less nervous," Amelia said. "What do we do if it breaks out? Will it eat me?"

"They are mainly carnivorous, but it's very unlikely that it'll eat us," Chris said.

"'Very unlikely' isn't reassuring enough," Amelia said.

"If it escapes, run. And don't let it catch you."

The lock case was loosening. Another minute or so and they'd have the lock and handle out of the door. They worked feverishly, even though Amelia still wasn't clear why they were doing what they were doing. Surely they should be securing themselves somewhere rather than making it easier for someone to get in. With the lock and handle gone the only way to keep the door closed would be to lean up against it, otherwise anyone could easily push it open. She hoped Chris knew what he was doing.

There was another growl from the badger room opposite. The growl reminded her that all that stood between them and a scary animal was a wooden crate that was a lot flimsier than she would have liked.

"Just hang in there, Claws," Chris whispered.

"Did you just give it a name?" Amelia asked.

"Yes, Claws O'Toole. I think it suits him," Chris said.

He's definitely not himself, Amelia thought.

Downstairs, Sam and Brian were feeling the strain. They didn't know how much longer they could keep the two men out of the house. Lionel had his shoulder in the small of Burt's back. He shoved his brother forward.

"Easy, Lionel, you're squashing my guts."

Lionel ignored him. They were gaining a few inches with every passing minute. Now, Burt's face was pressed up against the door, distorting his features. He swore wildly, inventively, and unintelligibly.

"Let us in," Lionel said. "We don't want to hurt you. We just want to take what's ours."

"You mean . . . the badger?" Brian said.

"So, you've seen that, huh? Vicious little guy. Nearly took my brother's hand off."

Lionel gave a tremendous shove and the door opened another little bit. Half of Burt's belly jiggled into view.

"Just to be clear, it's not illegal to own an exotic pet in

Ireland," Lionel said. "There's no law against it. You're the ones breaking the law here."

Brian didn't know if that was true, but even if owning an exotic pet wasn't against the law it was wrong. And stealing the creature from its homeland had to be wrong, too.

They weren't going to be able to hold out much longer. Sam gave a grunt and tried his best to force the fridge forward. It didn't make any difference. Lionel and Burt were too strong for them. It was men against boys. They were almost in now.

Lionel stopped for a moment when he peered over Burt's shoulder and recognized Brian. "Wait a second, I *thought* it was you again. Why do you keep turning up everywhere we go? What's your problem with us? All we're trying to do is make a living."

"By stealing," Brian panted.

"When we get in there, you're going to pay for emptying that bottle of soda over my head," Burt said.

"I really . . . enjoyed that. Made you . . . look like an idiot. Although that was . . . easy . . . since you're already . . . halfway there."

He knew he shouldn't have said it, but he couldn't help himself. It only spurred the brothers on.

"That . . . wasn't . . . helpful," Sam groaned.

"You're dead," Burt said.

"Don't you get . . . tired of saying that? You really need

to come up . . . with some new threats," Brian said. "Show a bit of imagination."

"Would you . . . please stop . . . antagonizing them," Sam wheezed.

They heard scraping sounds coming from upstairs, as if Amelia and Chris were moving a fridge up there, too. They had no idea what was going on, but less than a minute later, when Brian and Sam were on their very last legs, Amelia appeared beside them. She was carrying a push broom she'd found. She began to poke Burt in the belly with the tip of its handle.

"Stop it," Burt yelped.

"You ready?" she asked Brian and Sam.

They twisted as much as they could until they were looking up at her.

"Yeah," Sam said.

"Then move."

She flipped the broom around and then pressed the head, with all its soft bristles, in Burt's face. He spluttered and jerked backward, losing a little ground. Amelia dropped the broom, turned, and raced away. Brian and Sam weren't sure what she was up to, but they followed her.

As they reached the stairs, they heard Lionel and Burt pushing the fridge back. Moments later, they were in the house.

Brian had only made it to the second step when he saw the wooden crate sitting at the top of the stairs. That was the scraping sound they'd heard—Chris and Amelia had moved it into position.

Amelia squeezed between the crate and the banister. Sam followed her. Brian was the last to slip through the gap and into the upstairs hall, just as Lionel and Burt arrived below.

They stopped dead and looked up at the Misfits standing above them.

"What are you going to do? Push the crate down on top of us? Do you really think that's going to wor—"

Amelia and Chris gave the heavy crate a single shove. It slipped over the lip of the top step. Gravity took over and it tumbled down the stairs. Amelia saw the fear on Lionel's and Burt's faces before they took swift evasive action by running toward the front door.

"Follow me," Chris said to Sam and Brian. He turned to Amelia. "Are you sure about this?"

"I'm the fastest," she said.

Lionel dialed a number on his phone.

"We have them trapped, but we need your help," he said into the phone, before ending the call.

The crate lay at the bottom of the stairs. The lid had popped off and jewelry, artwork, and several antique pieces that the brothers had stolen over the last few months had spilled out onto the grimy floor. Burt walked across the different piles of necklaces and bracelets and jade earrings and kicked an antique clock out of his way. His foot tore through the canvas of a painting from a Dutch master. He shook it off and angrily flung the painting back toward the front door.

When Lionel looked up, there was no sign of any of the Misfits.

He pushed Burt ahead of him.

"Why do I have to go first?"

"Ugliest ones always go first," Lionel said.

They climbed the stairs cautiously, wary of another crate bouldering down. There wasn't a sound. Nobody was moving up there. The men looked at each other and took deep breaths. What were they waiting for? It was only a bunch of kids they were up against.

They reached the landing. Still no sign of anyone. The second crate was in the hallway, blocking the door to the first room off the landing, the room with the fireplace where Brian had found the two crates. There was just enough space to squeeze by and continue down the hall to the other two rooms, but Burt would have to suck in his stomach. Lionel nodded to his brother. The kids could be hiding in that fireplace room using the crate to block the doorway in a pathetic attempt to keep them out. If they were in there, they were trapped.

Lionel nodded to Burt, a signal to move the crate out of the way. Before Burt could get started, they both heard the urgent whispering coming from the end of the hallway.

Lionel took a step forward, the floorboard creaked, and

the whispering stopped. He smiled to himself. There was nowhere for the children to go. The only way they could leave the room without having to pass him in the hall was by leaping out of the window and they weren't going to do that.

Another five or six steps and he'd be there. *Dumb kids,* he thought. *Why did they think hiding up here was a good idea?*

They reached the end of the corridor and looked to the badger room on the left. The creature wasn't going crazy in its crate, so that meant the kids weren't in that room, Lionel reckoned. Whoever had been doing all the whispering was in the bright blue room on the right.

The door to that room was wide open. The men had a clear view of the retina-burning blue inside. There was no sign of anyone, but the window was open.

"On the ledge," Burt whispered. He nodded in the direction of the window.

Lionel didn't agree. If they were on the ledge, they'd see them, wouldn't they? Even if they were hanging by their fingertips? Surely, they hadn't jumped down . . .

Amelia hadn't jumped. She was less than six feet away, hoping the men wouldn't hear her heart thumping against her rib cage. She was pressed against the wall of the blue room, hidden in the small gap between the wall and the open door.

Lionel took a step toward the window, just to make sure.

He craned his neck and looked out. "They're not there," he whispered.

When Amelia was certain the men had stepped far enough into the room, she began to creep out. As she pushed the door back in order to slip away, the hinges gave a little squeak.

Lionel heard her move and sighed. "We've locked the front door and we have reinforcements on the way. You might as well—"

Amelia was fast and had escaped into the hall and was gone before he'd turned around. Lionel was about to take off after her when he was halted in his tracks. He saw something in the badger room across the hall that confused him. Chris was sitting on top of the honey badger's crate. The bottom three bolts were opened; he had his hands on the top two.

"What are you doing?" Lionel asked.

Chris didn't answer. Before Lionel or Burt could move, he'd slipped the final bolts from their receivers, then swung the door of the crate open.

"No!" Burt cried.

Farther down the hall, Brian and Sam had emerged from where they'd been hiding—behind a crate in the fireplace room—and pushed that crate forward, until it toppled through the door. It was just large enough to block the hall. There was no way to get from the badger or blue room at the end of the hall back to the stairs without climbing over it.

The honey badger growled softly as it click-clacked across the hall, pausing briefly to glance around before heading for the blue room where Lionel and Burt were frozen to the spot.

"Shut the door," Lionel screeched.

With the creature so close, Burt didn't want to get too near to it. He stuck out a leg and kicked the door. It swung shut, hitting the frame, then slowly swung open again.

Lionel realized why it hadn't clicked shut—the handle and lock were missing. Someone had taken them. Amelia and Chris.

"There's a good boy," Burt said. "Nice honey badger."

There was nothing to keep the creature out of the room now and it stalked in, baring its vicious little teeth as the two men backed away.

They did the only thing they could think of. They headed for the window ledge. They climbed out on the sill, two stories above the yard and, balancing precariously, pulled the window shut just as the creature raced toward them. They were safe.

The badger stared out the window at the two men.

They were safe, but they were trapped.

Chris sprinted from the badger room and into the hall. He was moving fast as the last thing he needed was to attract the creature's attention. He leaped onto the crate that was blocking the hall and Sam and Brian grabbed his arms and hauled him over to the other side, where Amelia was waiting. He didn't have to worry about being pursued. The badger's eyes never left Lionel and Burt, not even for a second.

THIRTY-ONE

The Misfits ran downstairs and out into the farmyard. Brian made sure they pulled the front door shut behind them. He checked it three times. The badger was safely locked in.

"Hey, kids, yeah, you. You can't just leave us up here," Lionel shouted.

The criminal brothers were on the windowsill, gripping the edges of the pebble-studded wall to stop themselves from falling to the yard below. Neither of them were looking in the window. They didn't want to remind themselves of what was in there. They could hear the badger clawing at the window of the blue room and it made their blood run cold.

Lionel reached out to see if he could grab the rusty drainpipe that ran down the side of the house. It was just a little too far. He tried again, but when he almost lost his balance he gave up.

"What are we going to do?" Brian asked. He was shaking. He still hadn't calmed down. Neither had Sam. He was more hyper than any of them had ever seen him.

"We've got two criminals on a window ledge, a honey badger in a farmhouse, and if our parents catch us we'll be grounded for a hundred years. Man, I feel alive," Sam said.

"Well, my hands are clammy, my pulse is twice the normal healthy rate, and I feel like I'm going to be sick," Amelia said.

"Exactly. Aren't adventures great?"

"We have to make sure that Claws O'Toole is okay," Chris said.

"Who's Claws . . . Oh, right, got it," Sam said. "Yes, we will, but first we're going to do something that you've always wanted us to do, Chris: call Debra."

"I thought you did that already," Chris said. "I told you to. I was quite specific about it."

"How was I supposed to call her when I was doing everything I could to stop those two bubbleheads from getting through the front door?"

"Well, *I* couldn't call—I had to come up with a plan to save Claws."

"So nobody called her?" Amelia said. "Maybe instead of bickering we could call her now."

"I'll do it," Sam said.

Lionel's voice floated over to them. "Hey, come on, kids. We weren't ever going to hurt you. Have a heart. There must be a ladder around here or something."

Burt wasn't saying anything. He was just whimpering to himself.

Sam dialed Debra O'Loughlin's number.

"She won't believe you," Brian said. "First a ghost, now a badger. I know he's vicious and all, but if someone told me they were being attacked by a badger I wouldn't believe them."

"That's why I'm not going to tell her the truth," Sam said.

Lionel was still shouting in the background, so Sam went into the empty milking shed to make the call. He checked around to make sure no one was listening. When Debra answered the phone, he put on a deeper voice, pretending that he was a grown man. He knew Amelia was right, that Debra wouldn't believe *him*, but she might believe him if she thought he was someone else. It was another perfect Trick Whittington moment.

"Hello, I'd like to report an incident at a farmhouse," he said.

"What's the address?" Debra O'Loughlin replied.

Sam read out the address from the printout Chris had given him.

"There's been a robbery—a burglary. And somebody's injured. Attacked by a dog. Three dogs. So, we'll need a wildlife expert, too."

"I see. It sounds serious."

"It is. Very serious."

"What's really going on, Sam?" Debra asked.

Sam reverted to his own voice. "How did you know it was me?"

"First of all, that fake voice of yours is ridiculous—far from convincing. And, secondly, you're calling me from your own phone. The name *Sam* came up on my caller ID."

Sam was a little deflated. That hadn't been his smartest move.

"I'm on the way to a case, so tell me what's happening," Debra said.

This time he told her and she believed him. Well, she believed him when she'd spoken to all the others and received the photos they'd texted her of Lionel and Burt stranded on the windowsill.

"I'm thirty minutes away—I'll be there in twenty," she said.

While they waited for Debra to arrive, Amelia called Hannah. She was thrilled to hear from them, shocked to hear about the badger and the stolen items in the crate at the bottom of the stairs, and delighted that everything was working out well. But she was bitterly disappointed that she hadn't been part of it.

"Stupid grounding," she said, over and over again. "I wait years for a mystery and then I miss the end of it. How's that for bad luck?"

Amelia did her best to reassure her that they would have

failed if it hadn't been for her, and when the others chimed in with their thanks she felt better.

Lionel yelped as the badger leaped in the air and clawed at the window again, scratching grooves into the glass. "Come on, man, you've got to help us. I don't know how long that window's going to hold."

Amelia said her good-byes to Hannah when they heard a car rumbling down the road.

"Debra's here," Brian said. "She must really have believed you this time."

The car that arrived in the yard wasn't a patrol car, though. It wasn't a car any of them had seen before. It was a nondescript black hatchback, driven by someone who looked vaguely familiar to Brian, even though the driver's face was obscured by a hoodie.

The car crossed the large yard and came to a stop by Lionel's Subaru as Amelia's phone rang. It was Hannah again.

"Put me on with Brian. Quickly," she said.

Amelia handed the phone to Brian. "It's Hannah."

"Okay, don't freak out, but I was going through the photos from the party on my dad's phone. That necklace Amelia found, the one that was in the attic in the cottage. There's a woman wearing it in one of the photos. You'll never guess who it is."

"My dad's girlfriend, Sharon," Brian said.

"How did you know?"

Brian didn't bother answering. He just handed the phone back to Amelia as the door of the car opened and Sharon Lachey climbed out. He couldn't say another word. He was in shock.

"We're up here, Alex," Lionel shouted.

Alex? Why are they calling her Alex? Amelia wondered. She thought the woman's name was Sharon.

"The badger's in the room. We can't go back in. He prefers attacking men to women, if you know what I mean," Burt called. "We're trapped."

Sharon didn't bother looking in the direction of her brothers. "Who have they called?"

"I couldn't hear what they were saying, but they made a couple of calls. Could you park the car under us? We can get dow—"

"Take out your phones, place them on the ground, and kick them over to me," Sharon, or Alex, said to the Misfits.

"If you think we're going to do—" Sam began.

Skraaaaak was the sound Chris's phone made as it slid across the yard and landed at Sharon's feet. He'd kicked it across immediately.

Sam sighed. "I see the old Chris is back."

"Sorry," Chris said, looking sheepish.

"What are you doing, Sharon?" Brian asked. "Is someone putting you up to this? Have they threatened you?"

"Threatened her?" Lionel cackled. "No one threatens our sister."

"Your *sister?* Sharon's your *sister?*"

"Well, it looks like the Scooby-Doo gang aren't as smart as they thought," Lionel said with a sneer.

"We're not the ones trapped on a window ledge by a honey badger, buddy," Sam said.

"When I get down there—"

"Shut up, Lionel," Sharon said. "Brian, I don't want to hurt you or your friends. I like your dad, and you were tolerable enough. I just want to take what's mine. I'll move on and we can all get on with our lives."

"You left the message in the hallway, the one warning me. That's why you only left it at my house. You'd have looked suspicious sending that to any of the others. You realized we were investigating that night at the party and dumped the necklace you were wearing so we wouldn't suspect you and—"

"This isn't a discussion, Brian. Just do what I say and everything will be fine."

"There's four of us and there's only one of you," Brian said.

"Do I appear to be worried about that?" Sharon replied.

Brian looked into her eyes and he knew she meant business. She was a different person from the one who'd been in his home. She held herself differently; she spoke differently. Had she been acting all the time? He realized he'd never known her. He'd never paid enough attention.

Without warning, Amelia sprinted toward Sharon, head down, charging like a bull. Sharon stepped to her left, dodging the attack. She grabbed Amelia by the collar and held her at arm's length.

"That was weak, kid. You really embarrassed yourself there," Lionel shouted gleefully. "Nobody messes with Alex Lambert."

"Is that your real name?" Brian asked.

Sharon looked annoyed that Lionel had unnecessarily revealed her full name, but she let it pass.

"It's not my intention to hurt anyone, but I will if I have to," she said. "Kick over the rest of the phones."

"There's still three of us and there's only one of her. We can do this," Sam whispered.

"What about Amelia? She might hurt her," Brian replied. "And you know what Chris is like. If he tries anything, he's probably going to get hurt. You don't want to do that, do you?"

"No, nobody hurts my brother except me."

"Phones now, unless you want to be responsible for your little friend being in pain," Sharon said, tugging at Amelia's collar.

"Don't worry about me. I'll be fine," Amelia said.

"I said *now*," Sharon growled.

Reluctantly, Sam and Brian did as they were told—they kicked the phones across the yard. Still holding on to Amelia,

Sharon stamped on each one in turn with the heel of her boot, until they were all smashed up and unusable.

Chris looked as if he was about to cry. He really loved that phone.

"It's very simple. We're going to go into the house and rescue the two men on the windowsill—"

"Thanks, sis," Burt said.

"—we're going to take the badger, and then we're going to leave. I'll lock you in the house and I'll call the police personally in a few hours to make sure you've been released. I'll be on my way and we'll never have to see each other again."

"You act like you're all civilized, but you're not, you know. You're horrible," Chris said. "Why would anyone want to steal a poor little honey badger?"

"I didn't. That was down to Dumb & Dumber up there," Sharon said.

"It's no big deal," Burt said. "Some obnoxious rich kid wanted a vicious, ferocious animal for his birthday party, like it'd be a cool thing to show off to all his friends, so we got him one."

"Except he didn't want a flippin' badger, though, did he?" Lionel said.

"Not this again," Burt moaned.

"He wanted the world's most fearsome animal, something like a lion or a tiger or a rhinoceros, I guess, but Alfred

Einstein here googled the world's most fearless animal instead. Turns out that was a honey badger."

"I made a mistake, right. Anyone can make a mistake."

"Yeah, 'cause when you want a lion at your party and you get a badger instead, that's a normal kind of mistake."

"Shut up, Lionel."

"You shut up, Burt."

"Both of you shut up," Sharon snapped. "The kid is going to take the badger and he's going to like it. And it's *Albert* Einstein. Imbeciles."

She released Amelia, giving her a gentle shove forward. "Get back to your friends," she told her.

"We can still do it," Sam whispered.

"Don't even think of trying to stop me. If you do, then I might have to implicate someone else in my crimes. Understand what I'm saying, Brian?" Sharon said.

Brian wasn't always the quickest on the uptake, but he understood immediately. If he stopped her and she was arrested, she was going to lie and tell the police that Mucky was involved in all of this. His father was many things, but he certainly wasn't a thief. Brian's blood began to boil.

"I'm going to assume you've called the cops," Sharon said. "They won't be coming for some time. I've reported a number of fake crimes at various locations a little off the beaten track. The Newpark police have never been so busy. So just do what I say and forget any ideas you might have of the cavalry coming to the rescue—"

She stopped talking when she heard the car approaching. It was nearing twilight and the driver had switched the dipped headlights on. The beams jolted around as the car bounced up and down on the narrow, rutted path that led to the farmhouse. "What was that you were saying about the police?" Sam said smugly.

But the car that arrived in the farmyard wasn't a police car this time either, and it wasn't driven by Debra O'Loughlin. It was a big old battered jeep that had seen better days.

"Who's that?" Sam asked.

"That's my gran," a stunned Amelia said.

THIRTY-TWO

Florence Parkinson was behind the wheel of the jeep, and Hannah was in the passenger seat. The vehicle came to a shuddering stop. Florence climbed out slowly, leaning heavily on the door for support.

"Touch of arthritis," she said. "I should get a smaller car at my age, but I love this old jalopy."

Sharon, who'd remained cool, calm, and collected even when she'd seen her own brothers trapped on a window ledge, seemed a little taken aback when she saw Florence.

"Now, what's going on here?" Florence asked. "Hannah said that Amelia, Derek, and all the boys were in some sort of trouble."

Hannah raced over to the rest of the gang.

"I'm so dead," she said, laughing. "I snuck out of my bedroom window and got your gran to drive me here. I don't care what happens to me tomorrow. I had to be part of it. I couldn't miss out on all the action."

She hugged Amelia, but let her go when she realized Amelia wasn't hugging her back. In her excitement, she hadn't noticed the woman standing ten yards away. She looked at her for a moment, a little confused. Then it dawned on her.

"That's Sharon."

"Yes," Amelia said. "Except her name's not Sharon. It's Alex."

"She's not trapped like the other guys?"

"No. And they're not just some other guys—they're her brothers."

"So, you mean . . . Oh."

She quickly scanned her surroundings and realized something.

"I understand that the two men on the ledge are some class of burglar, because Hannah filled me in on some of the story, but she was talking quite quickly, so I might not have grasped all of it. Is that Sharon, the girl Mucky's stepping out with?" Florence said.

Sharon looked at her brothers, then looked at the Misfits. Things were getting out of hand. There were too many people involved and the police wouldn't stay away forever. It had become complicated. Sharon had one rule, a rule that had kept her out of prison for many years: When things get complicated—leave.

"Alex?"

Lionel couldn't believe it when he saw his sister heading for the car. She stopped for a moment, looking for her keys. When she didn't find them immediately, she swore.

"What are you doing? Don't leave us here," Burt shouted.

"She's running away," Sam said.

He was filled with a sudden unfiltered energy and he didn't know what to do with it. He couldn't chase after her, not if it meant getting Brian's dad in trouble. Instead, he jumped up and down.

Hannah hadn't heard the threat though and she wasn't about to let Sharon escape. Not after everything they'd been through.

She shouted to Florence, "Get in the car and start it up."

Florence, who never normally took orders from anyone, was so taken aback that she climbed in. She was slow, but just fast enough for what Hannah had planned. Hannah jumped in the passenger side as Florence started the jeep. Sharon finally found her keys and climbed into her car.

"Reverse, Florence, reverse."

"I always have difficulty finding reverse . . . Ah, there we are. Where are we going?"

"There's only room enough for one car on the road out. If we reverse and block it—"

"She won't be able to get past and she can't escape by car. Got it. So, she's one of the baddies, too, then."

Florence reversed fast, the jeep bouncing against the hedge on one side of the narrow path, then the other, before a side mirror snapped off.

Sharon's black hatchback raced across the yard. Chris had to jump out of the way. When Sharon saw that her only exit was blocked by the jeep, she honked the horn in a futile gesture. Florence and Hannah waved at her cheerfully.

They both had the same thought. Florence handed the keys of the jeep to the young girl.

"You want me to do it?" Hannah said.

"We can't open the doors because we're too close to the hedges. And I'm not built for climbing out of windows now, am I, dear?"

Hannah rolled down the passenger window as Sharon climbed out of her car, a thunderous look on her face. Before she could reach Hannah, the young girl had slipped out of the window and pulled herself up onto the roof of the jeep.

"What's she doing?" Amelia asked.

Hannah stood there, right in the middle of the roof, looking defiant.

"That'd be a very stupid thing to do," Sharon warned her.

"I'm a Misfit. I do stupid things all the time," Hannah said.

She flung the keys of the jeep as far away as she could. They sailed over the hedge and deep into the thick, lush grass of the uncut field. It would take hours to find them in daylight, but now, as night approached, it would be impossible.

The Misfits Club cheered. They cheered again moments later, when they heard the faint sounds of a patrol car's siren on the main road.

With no way of escaping by car and the police approaching, Sharon had only one chance left. She set off on foot toward the fields at the back of the house.

The siren spooked Lionel and Burt, too. This time, it was Lionel's turn to whimper.

"I don't want to go back to prison," he said.

"Should we follow her?" Brian said. He didn't know what to do. He was furious with her, but he couldn't risk getting his dad in trouble. Could he?

Florence poked her head out of the jeep's window. "Don't even think about it, Derek. You've done enough—don't push your luck."

"She's right," Amelia said. "She won't get far."

The siren drew closer and, shortly after, they heard the car traveling down the narrow path.

"It's like Piccadilly Circus around here," Florence said.

Burt was spooked. "I'm not getting arrested. I'm escaping, too," he said. "I can make the car."

The Subaru Impreza was about ten yards away from the ledge. If Burt hoped to land on its roof to break his fall, it was going to take a superhuman leap.

"You won't make it," Lionel said. "It's too far to jump."

The patrol car came to a stop directly behind Florence's jeep.

Burt was ready. "I'm going on the count of three," he said, summoning up his courage. "One and two and—"

Burt didn't make the car.

Debra O'Loughlin had to climb over the roof of the jeep to get into the yard. After a quick and confusing briefing from all five club members, she radioed for backup and set off after Sharon.

The next couple of hours were chaotic. Florence's jeep was pushed out of the way to make room for all the cars that were coming and going. Sergeant Macklow and Tim/Jim were among the first to arrive and found it difficult to take charge of the situation. Everything was so confusing. They were more used to dealing with crimes like shoplifting and were both glad when Debra arrived with Sharon in handcuffs shortly afterward. Macklow allowed her to run the show.

"It'll be good for you to gain some experience," he said.

A local farmer brought a ladder and Lionel was rescued and then swiftly arrested. The last anyone saw of Burt was when he was being loaded into an ambulance, with his arms strapped up and splints on both of his legs. He was weeping quite a bit.

Later in the evening, a wildlife expert arrived and after some tense moments managed to sedate the honey badger. It was taken away and given a full checkup and found to be in surprisingly good health, to Chris's relief.

"We did it! We actually did it!" Amelia cried, punching the air.

"We did. Though I'm still not really clear on what

happened," Sam said. "Or why someone wanted a honey badger as a pet."

"Don't worry about it. I'll explain it all to you in a *lot* of detail when we get home," Chris said.

"Great, that's something to look forward to," Sam said.

"So, that's it," Hannah said with a smile. "We've solved our very first mystery."

"And it was a big one," Brian said.

They hugged—except for Sam, who tried to remind them that Misfits should never hug, but was ignored—and exchanged fist bumps and high fives.

Florence ambled over. "Hannah, your parents are here," she said.

Hannah had been dreading meeting her mother again. She was expecting her to shout and roar and ban her from leaving the house for life, but instead her reaction was quite different.

"Oh, my precious angel," Mrs. Fitzgerald said, grabbing her daughter and squeezing her so tightly Hannah could hardly breathe.

"You're smothering me," Hannah gasped.

"I know, I know. I can't help it. I just worry about you so much. You mean the world to me and I'm always terrified something bad will happen to you. I'm too protective. I can see that now. It's not making you happy living with so many rules and regulations—that's why you're taking all these risks. We can try and compromise, find a way that works for all of us."

"No, I mean you're smothering me with this hug."

"Oh," her mother said, laughing and crying at the same time. She released her grip on Hannah. As soon as she was free, her father grabbed his daughter in a bear hug. Big, fat tears rolled down his face. Hannah had never seen either of them behave like this before. She wondered if they'd gone insane.

"What have you been up to, you foolish, brave girl?"

"Having fun," Hannah said. "Why aren't you angry?"

"I am angry, but I'm proud, too, and . . . just so happy you're okay. Come on, we're taking you home," Mr. Fitzgerald said.

"Any chance we could stop for fries?" Hannah said. "I know they're not healthy, but—"

"You can eat fries until you're sick," Mr. Fitzgerald said.

Sam and Chris's parents were less pleased with their sons' activities.

"But, Dad, we foiled a criminal gang," Chris pleaded.

"Well, let me tell you, that's the last foiling either of you two will be doing for a very long time," their father said. "No more action movies for you, Sam, and, Chris, say good-bye to your computer."

"That's not fair."

"You think that's not fair? I'm only getting started," their dad said.

"They'll all calm down eventually, in a year or two," Florence said to Amelia and Brian when the twins had been taken home. "You do realize you were very foolish, don't you?"

"In my defense, I'm not smart enough not to be foolish," Brian said.

"And you always said I was too uptight. See what happens when I'm not uptight?" Amelia said.

"Yes, I can imagine your father will be delighted when he hears that you've got some of your old grandmother's spirit," Florence said.

"You're not going to tell him, are you?" Amelia said.

"Of course I'm not," Florence said. "You are."

Since Florence's car was out of action until the following day, Debra gave them a lift home. She put Brian's bike in the trunk—the other bikes would have to be collected later. Debra was in good spirits and couldn't hide it. After she'd reassured Brian that Mucky wasn't going to get in any trouble, she told them all how she chased Sharon through the fields and rugby-tackled her to the ground.

"She was no match for me." She beamed. "It was like I was on *Criminal Minds* or something. It was amazing."

Amelia and Florence were dropped off first and said their good-byes.

"Make sure you come over for lunch tomorrow, if you're free," Florence said to Brian as she exited the car.

"I'd like that," Brian replied. "Good last adventure, huh?"

"Doesn't have to be the last one," Amelia said.

"What do you mean?"

"Hannah's still here and I think I'll be visiting a lot more, too. And though you think of yourselves as detectives, none of you seem to have noticed how much Horace wants to join your club. He drops hints every time he sees you."

"He does?"

"And there's nothing stopping Sam and Chris from starting up a Galway branch of the club and meeting up from time to time."

"Yeah, we could go international."

"Galway isn't intern—Never mind. Things change, but it's not always the worst thing, you know. At least, not in my experience," Amelia said. "See you tomorrow. Misfits rule, right?"

Brian smiled. "Yeah, Misfits rule," he said.

AMELIA'S JOURNAL

I thought when I was being kicked out of the house that I'd hate it at my gran's, but I couldn't have been more wrong. She's much cooler than I thought and I've had the most amazing adventure and made the best friends. They are nothing like my friends at home—let's face it, they're a little bit odd, but then, so am I. I didn't know that before. What's so bad about that, anyway?

Gran made me call my dad and tell him what was going on. He shouted A LOT. But he wasn't really mad at me. He was mad at Gran for some reason even though I was the one who'd done all the things he was mad about. Gran didn't seem to mind him shouting down the phone at her. She just kept reading the newspaper and saying, "Yes, dear" from time to time. The worst thing is that now I have to go back home again, away from here and away from my new friends. That's such a pain. If I heard someone had stopped a load of crimes, I'd be saying well done and giving them free food and movie vouchers and new clothes and stuff like that. I wouldn't be punishing them. NO WAY!

The good thing is that while Dad was wandering around the house shouting a lot, Vivienne got on the phone. We actually had a nice talk. I said sorry for what I'd done and promised to help more and she said sorry, too. She said she'd let me think they sent me away because I was annoying them, but really she was just finding things tough at home and she thought it best if I went away for a while rather than see her all stressed and stuff. I think we might be friends again. She started telling me about Susanna and she sounds different from when I left. I didn't think that babies could change much in such a short time, but Vivienne says she has and why would she lie? I think I'm actually looking forward to seeing Susanna again. That's strange, isn't it?

I'm going to bed now. It's been a long day. I still can't believe what we've done. Sometimes it doesn't seem real and then other times it does and I feel all excited and panicky at the same time. The story was even on the news on the radio (no television at Gran's. Grrrrr). It said that Sharon—her real name is Alex Lambert, Sharon is an alias—had been stealing stuff like jewelry and paintings in America for years and years, but the police there had almost caught her, so she came home to Ireland and had been working here with her two brothers for the last six months. They'd found all these old properties and paid people to use them (people like Rodney O'Reilly—I wonder what will happen to him). They'd hide the stuff there until they were ready to move it out. They rented under false names so if anyone found the goods, then they'd be able to say it wasn't them or something like that. I'm sure Hannah and Chris will explain it all. That's if I'm ever allowed to see them again.

THIRTY-THREE

Brian was surprised to find Mucky sitting at the kitchen table when he got home. He was so used to him lying on the couch in front of the television that it looked all wrong to see him like this.

"You're late," Mucky said. "Are you okay?"

"Yeah, fine," Brian replied.

He wasn't used to being asked if he was all right, either. He sat down at the table.

"Did you hear about Sharon?" Mucky said. "Tom Moran rang me. Said some local boys caught her robbing animals from a farm or something. He didn't have all the details."

"I'm sorry," Brian said. And he was surprised to find he meant it. He wasn't sorry that she was gone, but he was sorry for his dad.

Mucky didn't seem to be fully aware of all the drama at the farmhouse or Brian's involvement in what had happened. He'd tell him later.

"Don't be sorry, I'm not. I'm kind of relieved, actually," he said with a smile. "So, ol' Shar was some kind of criminal genius."

"Not sure she was a genius."

"She was genius enough to outsmart me," Mucky said.

"And me," Brian said. She'd been right under his nose the whole time and he'd never suspected her.

"Guess the McDonnell boys aren't the brightest bulbs in the . . . um, you know, something or other."

"Guess not."

They both stared at the table for a few moments.

"Things were better when your mother was here, weren't they?"

"Yeah, they were," Brian said.

Mucky hadn't been too bad back then. Not great—he'd never been that; it wasn't in his nature—but he had been better.

"Maybe we could try and make them better again," Mucky said. He ran his fingers through what was left of his long, thin hair. "I think it's time we did things a bit differently around here. Not too much, mind. Too much change can be bad for you, but a little bit."

"I'd like that," Brian said.

Mucky got up from his chair. He looked happier, as if the conversation had made him feel better.

"Think I'll watch some TV and then go to bed," he said. He turned back. "We can watch something you're interested in, you know . . . if you like."

"No, you're good. Watch what you want, Dad."

"Great, that's great."

Brian heard the dual sounds of the television coming to life and Mucky settling into the couch with a satisfied sigh.

"Brian?"

"Yeah?"

"Sam, Chris, Hannah, and Amelia. They're your friends' names, right?"

"Yes, Dad, they're my friends."

He'd actually learned their names. That was progress, wasn't it? *Maybe Amelia's right after all*, Brian thought. *Maybe change isn't the worst thing in the world.*

THE NEWPARK ECHO

Thursday, August 26

EXCITEMENT IN EXCITING TOWN

Newpark, once ridiculed by the overrated travel writer William Wrydaughter as a cure for insomnia, was possibly the most exciting place on the planet for a few hours on Tuesday night. With honey badgers on the loose, criminals trapped on a window ledge, a dastardly illegal trade foiled, a local young police officer's reputation restored, and with some resourceful children at the heart of it all, there was barely time for this reporter to draw breath.

When the self-styled Misfits Club—consisting of local children Brian McDonnell, brothers Sam and Chris Adamu, Hannah Fitzgerald, as well as Amelia Parkinson, the granddaughter of Newpark native Florence Parkinson—went looking for the ghost of Patrick Grenham (excitement *and* a local ghost? Take that, Wrydaughter) they had no idea what they were about to discover. But thanks to a combination of bravery, intelligence, and good old-fashioned doggedness, these scrappy youngsters were able to unravel a web of mystery and save the day.

It is believed that the non-Newpark criminal gang

had been operating all over the country, but they made a big mistake when they set foot in the town with Ireland's only ketchup museum. The gang's leader, Alex Lambert, aka Sharon Lachey, has been responsible for the theft of rare items such as paintings and jewelry, as well as exotic pets, in America for years, but recently moved home to Ireland after being pursued by the US authorities. Lambert and her brothers allegedly stole unusual items to order and then sold them to rich buyers, but they met their match when they arrived in our fair town.

There were three arrests made that night by Officer Debra O'Loughlin, with further arrests expected to follow.

Sergeant Calvin Macklow was full of praise for O'Loughlin, who brought down the gang's leader: "She did a great job. We always knew she had it in her. She's rescued cats like Lumpy in the past; now she's rescuing badgers. At this rate, she'll be opening her own zoo."

And what of the honey badger? Claws O'Toole, as he has been unofficially named, is already on his way to a sanctuary on his home continent of Africa, where he will be well looked after. Cornelius Figg, Ireland's wealthiest man, has agreed to fund the cost of transporting Claws to Africa, as well as financing the running of the sanctuary for the next five years. According to Officer O'Loughlin, the criminals had Claws in their possession because they believed that Cornelius Figg wanted to purchase the world's most fearsome animal for his son Barney. In what was a criminal clerical error, the Lambert gang accidentally researched "world's most fear*less* animal," which led them to capturing the brave, and occasionally vicious, honey badger.

The whole enterprise was a misunderstanding according to Plunkett Healy, a spokesman for Mr. Figg: "Young Barney is an amazing, caring boy who innocently expressed an interest in working with wildlife at some point in the future. He never wanted to own such a beautiful creature. The honey badger belongs to nature, not to man."

What's next for the Misfits Club? Chris Adamu had this to say: "We promise to investigate crime, fight evil, and put ourselves in peril to right wrongdoings everywhere." Unfortunately for young Adamu, he may not get the chance to do any of this since he has been grounded for the next year.

OUR WILD FRIENDS NEED YOUR HELP

SUPPORT THE
WILD FRIENDS' FEDERATION

ACKNOWLEDGMENTS

I would like to say thanks to everyone at Macmillan publishers for all their support, especially my brilliant editor, Lucy Pearse. Thanks, as always, to my agent, Marianne Gunn O'Connor. And last, but never least, thanks to Dee, my first reader and best friend.